BONAVENTURE POINTE, A WESTERN ROMANCE

Beachcombing in a Liminal Zone of Postmodern Hyperreality

VOLUME 2

Konrad Ventana

iUniverse books may be ordered through booksellers or by contacting:

iUniverse
1663 Liberty Drive
Bloomington, IN 47403
www.iuniverse.com
844-349-9409

ISBN: 978-1-6632-5890-8 (sc)
ISBN: 978-1-6632-5891-5 (e)

Library of Congress Control Number: 2022921308

Print information available on the last page.

iUniverse rev. date: 03/23/2024

CONTENTS

Part 1. A Literary Chiasmus in Neo-Noir 1

Chapter 1 2
Chapter 2 15
Chapter 3 21

Part 2. Tending the Wounded Under Fire **35**

Chapter 4 36
Chapter 5 50
Chapter 6 60

Part 3. Epic Intercontinental Cliffhanger **77**

Chapter 7 78
Chapter 8 82

The solution of the difficulty is that the two mental pictures which experiment lead us to form—the one of the particles, the other of the waves—are both incomplete and have only the validity of analogies which are accurate only in limiting cases.

—Werner Heisenberg, ca. 1930

Summary of Volume 1, *The Benightment*

On an abandoned beach on the Southern California coast near midnight, Everett Durant reaches both hands into the pockets of his jeans as he approaches the water's edge. He unburdens himself of all his personal belongings as he prepares to commit suicide by drowning. But he fails. During his unsuccessful drowning, Everett experiences the appearance of a guardian angel of sorts. When he awakes, he sees only the impression of a sand angel remaining where he himself washed ashore.

Everett soon learns that a young girl either jumped or fell from the cliffs above and suffered and died not so long ago. This realization encourages the washed-up emo songwriter to honor her memory in a constructive way, which is what sets the saga in motion. Following his unsuccessful suicide by drowning, Everett's eyes are opened to the hopelessly disenfranchised homeless population around him, and he becomes the post-Beat poetic voice of a generation in tumult. He deeply connects with those considered to be the underbelly of society, giving homeless people a resounding voice through his collection of post-Beat poetry.

Soon, a quick fifteen minutes of fame lead him onto the path of Beatrice Rutherford, otherwise known as "the heiress." With the prompting of the heiress, Everett moves deeper into the disorienting seas of cultural conformity, mass socialization, and geopolitical control, while championing the role of an inspired individual. He could never have imagined that a road trip with Beatrice into the Big Sur wilderness would become an incredible journey of adventure, discovery, and healing arts amid the governing hyperrealities of these feverish postmodern times.

Bonaventure Pointe: A Western Romance, Vol. 1, ends with a landslide event. In "An Interlude," we find Everett Durant, the washed-up post-Beat protagonist, and Beatrice Rutherford the heiress, returning to Los Angeles in a chartered helicopter with their anticipated road trip in suspended animation.

PART I

A LITERARY CHIASMUS
IN NEO-NOIR

Chapter 1

It was a short trip from the rooftop heliport landing pad to the uppermost interior floor of the Westin Bonaventure Hotel. The elevator doors opened to reveal the posh interior of LA Prime, an ultraclassy, uberromantic steakhouse serving prime beef steaks, fresh seafood, and an award-winning selection of French and Californian wines, all accolades that meant a lot in this particular town.

The well-dressed elevator doorman bowed ceremoniously, first to Miss Beatrice, and then to Everett Durant, offering to stow his and then her luggage, then directing them to the guest washrooms in the manner of a butler in a silent movie.

Everett smiled as he handed over his travel suitcase with all his worldly belongings to this reticent stranger, albeit one dressed in a fancy black tuxedo.

Upon Everett and Miss Beatrice's return to the dining room, a stylish hostess came forward to usher the late-night travelers to a reserved table, set elegantly for two, right in front of an imposing span of plate glass windows overlooking the greater LA metropolis, if not the whole wide world.

To Everett, the postmodern hostess, identifying as a female in terms of raiment, appeared to be a young, attractive, statuesque, platinum-blonde ingénue wearing a form-fitting miniskirt in the manner of a retro airline flight attendant, as if having shopped the cosplay wardrobes of the jet-setters of a time gone by, yet the more likely scenario was that the stylish hostess of this outré Los Angeles dining establishment was an aspiring movie actress inadvertently auditioning to capture the attention of some assistant director or get an invitation to appear on a fully fledged director's casting couch while balancing precariously on high-fashion patent-leather ankle-strap platform pumps.

Everett politely held the seat out for Beatrice before taking his place at the white linen table, which had been elegantly prepared for them in advance of their arrival. Candles were lit.

Everett raised a freshly filled water goblet in a cordial salute to the heiress. "I'm impressed, Miss Beatrice. *The earth actually did move!* For both of us!" he said. "But I must say, Miss Bliss, I am still a bit unnerved by these abrupt changes in location and setting, and these god-awful memories that continue to haunt and distress me, not to mention this impossibly well-timed series of rainstorms, atmospheric rivers of water vapor, and localized mudslides that just happened to block US Highway 1 yet again, leaving your sporty Bentley Continental GT convertible standing all alone on a mountainside, stranded like our epic road trip among the far-reaching winds, the desolation angels, and latter-day dreams of beauty—stranded alone and trembling on the adamantine cliffs of what is literally and figuratively the island of Big Sur!"

Beatrice simply tilted her head sideways and smiled, beaming with a quiet confidence.

"Is it always like this with you, Miss Bliss? Does the earth actually move each time you embark on one of your illustrious road trips? Is *this* the mystical ecstatic shamanistic business that the distinguished visiting professor was attempting to warn me about over lunch in Santa Barbara?!"

"Don't be silly, Everett. I am nearly as surprised by the sudden landslides as you are. Although, on another level, the Big Sur environs have always been considered to be much like an island in many ways—historically, philosophically, and idealistically speaking, that is. On yet another level, Everett, I am interested to learn what you really think of Brother I-Heart."

"I like Brother I-Heart and his 'I Heart Jesus' outfit enormously," Everett responded without hesitation. "I mean, I'm enormously glad to have met the boldly bright and earnest young man." Everett nodded agreeably. "Brother I-Heart's sincerity and his humility are equally endearing to the likes of me, and his grasp of soulful expression is breathtaking."

"I'm so glad to hear you say that," said Beatrice. She signaled the hostess with a raised index finger. "Brother I-Heart certainly thinks the world of you, Everett. Somehow, I knew that it would be good—somehow I knew it would be important—for you to meet."

"Important for Brother I-Heart or *for me*?" asked Everett, his tone one of rising curiosity.

"For both, silly rabbit. For both of you. Teacher-and-student can be much like chicken-and-egg."

"Come to think of it," Everett said, "Brother I-Heart never did proffer his given name. Nor did he reveal the actual university that is supporting his research for his avant-garde dissertation." He pondered some more. "But I have a hunch, Miss Beatrice, that you might have an answer to these compelling academic questions."

Beatrice seemed bemused, and she chose her words carefully: "Brother I-Heart always keeps his given name strictly to himself, yet he considers his religious calling to be implicit." After a moment, she added flatly with a sly smile, "With that said, I can tell you that the boy currently hails from the Claremont University Graduate School of the Arts and Humanities. They do such wonderful work in the area of scholarship and antiquities."

Everett nodded and smiled. Inquisitively, he searched the heiress for more information.

"Yes, of course. I am providing financial support for collaborating high-minded academics, from the modern-day Library of Alexandria in Cairo, Egypt to the Coptic Studies Council right here in Claremont, California—including Brother I-Heart's bold New Testament studies in monasticism, iconography, liturgy, ministry, and sacred music."

"I see," said Everett. He lifted a water goblet, turning it reflectively to reveal its fine cut-glass facets. "I have a good feeling that Brother I-Heart is on the right track with his gnostic audio mixes and their potential application in religious services and concert venues. Choral orchestration can be very powerful emotionally." Returning the water goblet to the table, Everett raised his gaze to the vast metropolis of jewel-like lights gleaming in the silent spaces beyond the plate glass windows. "And yet above and beyond the obvious musical talents of the young man, which I can certainly appreciate, beyond the power of the enigmatic texts and codices perceived in humanistic terms, and beyond the longing vowels and chanting threads he sorts out on his electronic console for others to join in and experience collectively, I can tell you the bright young monk's desire to express himself in such an original way remains strong."

"I can agree with that, Everett," Beatrice said thoughtfully, fingering her angel kiss labret. "By the way, what did you think of Brother I-Heart's musical improvisations? You seemed to be enjoying yourself."

"Hey, no worries, Miss Beatrice. I have no complaints. Our road trip to Big Sur and beyond was a real good try," he said. "I enjoyed every minute of your company, and I appreciate your good intentions, pretty lady. I especially enjoyed the part where we were all busy parsing Coldplay's 'Paradise,' and Brother I-Heart was busy mixing audio threads, and the Big Sur hermitage monks were busy chanting for real, and the rain was busy pouring down, and suddenly the earth itself moved with a shuddering and imponderably symphonic rocking and rolling commotion."

"I remember the feeling, Everett. I was there with you. Remember?"

Their laughter was met by the arrival of the first course of what would turn out to be a veritable Rose Parade of culinary delights.

The stream of fresh seafood began with a sharing platter: crisp leaves of romaine beneath plump oysters on the half shell with grated Reggiano parmesan, shaved horseradish, cocktail sauce, and Tabasco. The platter of oysters went down easily and were followed by jumbo sizzling pan-seared sea scallops—*mano de leon*—giant, velvety, moist, golden porcini-crusted delicacies with a distinctive briny flavor that reminded Everett of the ocean.

"Lately it occurs to me, my enigmatic and mysterious designated driver, what a long, strange trip it's been for us already. But I want you to know, Miss Bliss, I am sincerely grateful for your good intentions and the brief, beautiful ride. Alas, it also occurs to me that our road trip to some kind remembrance has been permanently canceled on account of heavy rain."

"Did you notice how oppressive this storm has been? It has not abated since our road trip began!"

"Yes, I was there with you, remember?" Everett answered, repeating his companion's earlier reply.

"Do you also remember the Bible verses I shared with you on the lofty headland cliffs of Bonaventure Pointe, the sacred verses relating to the stinging locust allegory?"

"Yes, Beatrice. I remember you were quite upset about the *harm* they might possibly do."

"Not might do, Everett: *will do!*" Beatrice briefly stopped munching on her seafood to explain. "The legendary stinging locusts always do what they will. And they do harm!" she lamented. "They always have—for a specified period, that is. The dark vision I am trying to make clear for you Everett is that they are coming again!" Beatrice leaned in close to Everett and spoke in a whisper: "I can sense a veritable pandemonium of locusts coming along with this thoroughly inclement weather, Everett. We need to move quickly in terms of your deliverance, in terms of effectuating a larger saving grace."

"Saving grace, Beatrice? Are we both still on the same page here? I know you told me that we had something in common, that we have both been angelically touched." Everett pondered to recall the exact phrase. "Touched by the appurtenance of an angel. That's what you said. But I personally don't have any sixth-sense sentiments about any kind of locusts, Beatrice, be they stinging locusts with bad intentions or not!"

"What do I know, my tragic friend with the golden pen?" she said sarcastically. "I'm only a banker's great-granddaughter with an exceedingly rich cultural inheritance to work with!" Beatrice fluttered her eyelashes as she spoke. "Nevertheless, O poetic one, if you only knew how many people you would touch, and deeply, in the fullness of time." She paused briefly. "It's not only the wonderfully expressive words and songs you coauthored with Celeste Emo that moved me to reach out to you, Everett; it's also that voice of pure eloquence as expressed in the fabulous vagabond post-Beat poetry book you published subsequently, or rather gifted back." She paused again, smiling at the thought. "With your recent travels off the grid among the homeless, recorded in such a soaring postmodern backstreet patois, you gave a resounding, heart-wrenching voice to the most desperate of our countrymen, our countrywomen, and our lost children—the anguished souls, the poor in spirit, the grieving, the mad, the disabled, the distraught, the afflicted, and the abandoned souls—articulated with the crushing weight of disillusionment and dread that invariably plagues homeless people, including homeless children, abandoned by their own society."

Everett studied the timeless loveliness of the features on the face of the woman before him. She was gleaming in the flickering candlelight. Behind the artful, exaggerated makeup—that of the emotionally hard-core indie rock/emo fashionista trending toward scenester with the attractive angel kiss piercing that she wore so well—Everett could see an unmistakable tincture of sadness in her eyes beneath those dramatically dark black tresses and despite the concealing blush, the burnished-red lipstick, the smoky eyeliner, and the lash-lengthening mascara she wore.

"For pity's sake, Everett. I need to help you in the same way you helped me to resolve the coastal headlands development controversy—precisely, concisely, and wisely, simply by letting it be. Such lovely words of wisdom, Everett. They still mean a lot to me."

Everett smiled, acknowledging the lyrical line of her reasoning, yet he could sense that she still had pangs of a guilty conscience. The post-Beat lyrical poet thought for a long, intense moment, digging deep into his own tragic memories and his own grief, before finally striking emotional gold, able to offer up sympathetic words that might comfort the heiress who was grieving for her lost or abandoned children: "In China or a woman's heart, there are places no one knows," he intoned softly with a calm sense of assurance. Her face brightened as he spoke.

"Those are beautiful words, Everett. Did you write them?"

"They sure are beautiful words, but no, they're not mine."

"Did Stella—rather, Celeste Emo—write them?"

"No, ma'am. The best I can recall, the phrase was expanded from the title of a song by a lesser-known folk singer-songwriter named Kate Wolf, now departed—way too soon."

"Can you share more of Kate's song with me?" she asked. Her eyelashes fluttered invitingly.

Everett began singing melodically, "'Just a little box all covered with blossoms white as snow.'" He explained in some detail the story behind a little metal cloisonné box and the story behind that story. The box had come from the estate of the widow of a sea captain who lived on the prairie near Bartlesville, Oklahoma. When she died, they found that her home was completely filled with objects from the Orient, a place she'd never been. "'There were fancy silks and carved wood chests from the places he had gone,'" Everett sang. "'She kept them all until she died, but this was her favorite one.'" He paused for a beat before singing the chorus: "'Just a little box all covered with blossoms white as snow.'"

"Tell me more, Everett. Tell me all you can remember, even if it's only in fragments."

"Let's see," he began. "'It filled her heart with mystery and with magic on the day when he gave it to her for her own in his quiet, loving way.'" Everett continued in a modest falsetto: "'The treasures of her life were the things she left behind. They buried her without them where the prairie grasses grow. In China or a woman's heart, there are places no one knows.'"

"It's a very beautiful song, with such touching sentiments. Thank you for that," she said, casually brushing a tear from her cheek. "Did you happen to know the folk singer-songwriter personally?"

"No, I never met Kate Wolf in person. She shone brightly in the mid-1980s and died of complications from leukemia treatments at the age of forty-four, before my time in California. I was always a big fan of her folk-style poetry and her backroads ballads back then. I guess I still am. I know Stella, a.k.a. Celeste Emo, and I were both inspired artistically by Kate Wolf."

"How so, Everett? I'm really interested to know how that might work."

"Kate Wolf composed one of the most telling of all lyrical hooks: 'We've only got these times we're living in!'" Now, repeating the phrase, he said, "'We've only got these times we're living in!' The refrain is the artistic holy spur! And if she could, she'd tell us now, 'There are no roads that do not bend. And the days like flowers bloom and fade, and they do not come again.'"

"So terrifying and yet so true," the gossamer heiress stated conclusively.

The stylish hostess returned, the two guests selecting their entrées from an à la carte menu. The conversation moved on to the topic of the aforementioned train reservation, which was previously established as an alternative form of transportation.

"I can see our impending train ride represents some kind of mythopoetic bend in the road, Miss Bliss, and I'm kind of curious to find out exactly what kind of changes in course you are charting for our highfalutin road trip now."

"Oh, I can't possibly travel with you on the Angels Flight Railway. I don't have the slightest ability to pass through *that* eye of the needle, Everett. As much as I would like—make that love—to accompany you further and to go deeper together, my dear tragic poet and eloquent new friend, I simply don't have the sociopolitical sanctity, that is, the sanctity of original creativity, which is so evident in your tragic case, to do so." Beatrice stopped short of completing her off-putting explanation.

"What are you talking about, Beatrice? A tragic case, am I?" Everett frowned and shook his head. "Just when I was beginning to relax again and enjoy the ride, and just when I was beginning to trust that you might turn out be a reliable designated driver after all, you leave me hanging with a fancy final supper and a single train ticket to who knows where."

"I know precisely what I'm talking about, Everett Durant!" Beatrice declared. "And I am determined to help you in the ways that I am able. Seriously, I know what I am talking about, Everett, and I take some pride in being a reliable designated driver. It's just that these lofty issues, which border on the realm of the angelic, are still too difficult for me to discuss openly."

"I get you, Miss Beatrice. And I understand the difficulties involved when one's personal grief, humiliation, and shame are lit up by the mainstream media and strewn on the public beach like a gutless abalone shell—emptied out and busted, with a hole in the center the size of a stiletto's heel."

"Would it help you to trust me more if, perhaps, I shared something scandalous with you regarding my own angelic experiences? Would it enable you to feel more connected, less naked, and less emotionally exposed if we were to dare to share something angelic, something we would then have in common?"

"I can't promise anything, Beatrice. Especially if I don't know what you're talking about."

"It might help if I reminded you that your own much-publicized near-death experience, which bordered on angelic, happened to be context-dependent. I mean to say, it happened once upon a time, and it still reverberates within you—according to my due diligence, your own testimony, and the inspired messages that are evident in your own vagabond poetics, Everett."

"OK, Beatrice, I'll play along. Tell me about your impressions of such angels in the sand."

"Well now, I can't say too much about your particular angelic experience, Everett, because it's deeply personal, for you alone obviously. However, what I have learned from my recurring angelic experiences—in addition to contemporary readings from the Library of Alexandria and a lifetime of exercising due diligence as a fiscally responsible philanthropist—is that whatever is truly angelic in terms of saving grace is *not likely* to occur only once upon a time, Everett, dear."

"Recurring angelic experiences, you say? That does sound serious." He stroked his chin in the practiced manner of a post-Freudian psychotherapist. "And how does that make you feel, Miss Beatrice?"

"Please be serious, Everett."

"I was just dismissed as a tragic case. I thought you'd appreciate being seen from the same perspective."

"Fair enough. In your case and in my case, there is a vital connection between your singular angelic sighting and my recurrent angelic experiences, which are considered to be transgressive by some—perhaps by many."

"Good so far, Miss Bliss. I personally would rather be a vital connection than a clinical case study."

"The vital connection, I daresay, is that both our individual angelic appearances seem to be distinctly feminine in nature."

"And I suppose the idea of a female angel is the transgressive part you're fretting about?"

"Yes, exactly. And I know intuitively, if not instinctively, that my own visions and my own metaphysical places of refuge are more than likely related to the emergent manifestations of compassion associated with spiritual energy, according to Far Eastern philosophy, where a female spirit has been described as actively catching lost and falling children for a very long time now"—she covered her mouth discreetly with her hand, continuing in a whisper—"long before dear sweet Jesus lived and taught and nobly died, and before the beatific visions, the travelogues, and the memoirs of the apostles were canonized."

"What are you trying to tell me, Beatrice? Sure, I can understand my own confusion, having lived through what the newspapers touted humorously as an unsuccessful drowning experience. It's embarrassing; it's humiliating; and it's all out in the open now. Touched by the appurtenance of an angel, you say! Maybe so! Maybe so! One thing I can tell you about this guardian angel for certain: when she's with you, you'll surely know it, and when she's gone, you'll surely know that too!" He closed his eyes and cringed for a moment as he spoke. "Fleeting! That's all I know about guardian angels. Fleeting! That's what I learned from her salty kiss, Miss Bliss."

Their hostess uncorked a bottle of California chardonnay and then, after Everett had tasted it, poured two glasses. Next, the hostess formally presented a basket of sliced fruit and nut bread, pretzel sticks, lavash crisps, and ciabatta, also setting down a bowl of olive tapenade with red peppers, extra virgin olive oil, and balsamic vinegar. Next up was a tantalizing plate of pan-seared filet mignon Oscar with lump crabmeat, sautéed asparagus, and a rich béarnaise sauce, followed by a plate of tender roasted Chilean sea bass with Jerusalem artichoke puree, served with a drizzle of citrus emulsion and artfully garnished with tiny spring carrots, turnips, and radishes. Beatrice nodded appreciatively to the stylish hostess, waving her hand elegantly over the whole table, implying that the hostess should extend her compliments to the unseen chef.

"What I am proposing is an advantageous division of labor befitting our primary mission, that being you, Everett—specifically, the restoration and the redemption of *you*." Beatrice sliced deeply into the thick-cut filet mignon Oscar with the skill of a heart surgeon. "We can both agree that there are delicate chambers of the human heart that only a woman can fully appreciate, no?"

Everett speared a tiny spring carrot with his salad fork. He held it up for inspection, and smiled. "Hoisted with my own feminist petard, alas," he mumbled.

"And there are certain places where a rich and respectable socialite like me can never go?"

"But of course, Miss Beatrice. So, where am I, singular, headed off to? Where am *I* going that is considered taboo and thus off-limits to a beautiful, rich, and respectable woman of substance?"

Beatrice stopped chewing. She gracefully swallowed the bolus of steak Oscar, then took a sip out of the long-stemmed goblet, before responding to his query. "My role, Everett, is to prepare the way for you, not to walk your walk. However, if my travel plans for you go smoothly and both of us hold true to our intended purposes, we will meet again soon. To be specific, Manifesta et al. and I will meet you at the Henry Miller Memorial Library in Big Sur in a week or so—surely less than a month of Sundays from tonight."

"You mean *the* Manifesta, the fabulous Hollywood movie director? That Manifesta?!"

"There is but one Manifesta, Everett. And yes, she is fabulous—such an *ascension of the art*!"

"She is also wildly provocative, Beatrice. I've seen one of her public cinematic exhibitions in person, and I'm still shaken by the scorching CGI reenactments she flashed on the walls of public buildings. Wasn't Manifesta the one who holographically tied Marylin Monroe to the railroad tracks in downtown Los Angeles, filming onlookers walking by while Marilyn's naked body appeared, shimmering vividly in 3D, then disappeared, forcing the wide-eyed passersby to watch helplessly and thereby experience the proverbial plight of a damsel in distress?"

"That's my girl," Beatrice exclaimed in a somewhat ambiguous tone.

"The cinematic special effects she employs are exceedingly violent, Miss Beatrice," Everett said.

"There is a reason for that," Beatrice replied.

"Do tell," Everett pressed.

"As an auteur and feminist provocateur, Manifesta converts the existentialist's mythic fear of eternal recurrence into a contemporary dread of even more infernal reruns, using her high-tech art house engineering platforms as a force for revelation upon edification."

"That's a mouthful; needs some chewing," he said. "The dread of infernal reruns—I get that part. But revelation upon edification? You mean she shines bright lights on tall buildings?"

Beatrice brushed off his flimsy attempt at humor. "The director's hyperviolent oeuvre threatens to *rerun real events*, Everett, with ever-increasing cinematic intensity and gripping special effects. That is, at the same time she confronts the issues, she seeks redress for *the horrors* of celebrity-protected violence against women in Hollywood movieland, repeating those horrors by providing her audience with an alarmingly vivid audiovisual experience of the recurring nature of the reality."

"Manifesta's art house hyperreality platforms must be working, Miss Beatrice. It appears those nasty flash-style reruns of hers took down some well-deserving jerk-asses in Tinseltown and helped to clean up one of the raunchiest mean streets around. Still, I can't help but wonder what this fabulous, secretive, and reclusive Manifesta character has been up to lately. More to the point: I can't help but wonder what the Fabulous Manifesta character has to do with our fractured road trip, Miss Beatrice, but I'm guessing you might be able to tell me more about that."

"I can't talk about the former topic in the present tense, Everett; I have been sworn to secrecy. There is a forensic investigator currently in a witness protection program, and I'm very afraid I might blow his cover if I breathe a word about this to anyone. These are terribly dangerous times."

"OK. OK. I'm just curious. Let's simplify: what does any of this have to do with me?"

"Well. Do you remember the story about the SoCal fire chief who rose through the ranks of firefighters to eventually become fire captain and chief arson investigator—rising in social prestige to heroic status at a time when Southern California was experiencing an unprecedented outbreak of large, suspicious fires that damaged great swaths of land, only to identify the fire chief himself, in the end, as a serial arsonist and murderer, his having set these devastating fires as a ploy to promote his own celebrity?"

"I remember, Beatrice. But that's old news! So, this Smokey the Bear, this G-man, was actually the devious firebug! Call me way past any personal post-Freudian deliberations on impulse control, Miss Beatrice, but that's classic neo-noir in psychological terms. The theme goes back to Edgar Allan Poe's analysis in 'The Imp of the Perverse,' if you ask me. I think they even made a movie—"

"I repeat, I cannot say any more," Beatrice said, interrupting. Her appealing countenance flushed with an off-putting glower and a frown.

Realizing that his clumsy faux pas was not appreciated in the slightest, Everett finally got the message. "Oops, my bad. I didn't realize we were figuratively passing notes. What then can you tell me?"

"I can tell you that Manifesta and her Art House Studios just wrapped up an exhibition of the latest 3D holographic projection technology in Las Vegas. It's simply amazing to behold. Do you know that with the new computer-generated holography, one can experience Elvis Presley and/or Whitney Houston and/or Maria Callas performing live, onstage, on the same night?"

"I'm not sure where you're going with this, but I sure as hell don't want no holographic diva resurrected by Manifesta from the computer-generated netherworld to keep me company."

"I have no intention of simply entertaining you with Manifesta's virtual smoke and mirrors. I wouldn't dream of tricking or cheating you with such a cheap and hollow circus stunt. There is so much I want to share, but unfortunately, I can't say more. Manifesta made me promise."

The conversation was interrupted by the buzzing of Beatrice's cell phone, accompanied by a familiar constellation of musical chimes, which served to focus the cryptic conversation on the logistics of time, the difficulties of scheduling the VIP train trip, and the unspoken allure of the fabulous theatrical displays and dramatic exigencies remaining.

"I'm so sorry, but we might have to forgo the dessert menu, handsome." She raised her arm and motioned with an offhanded whirling of her fingers, signaling to the stylish hostess from a distance. "I do so enjoy our meals together, Everett, but we cannot afford to keep this fabulous director, or this particular train conductor, waiting."

"OK with me; I'm pleasantly filled," Everett remarked as he pushed back into his chair.

Less than a minute later, Beatrice's cell phone buzzed and chimed again.

"What's up with the pings?" he wondered out loud.

"That's our cue, Everett. Oh, this is so exciting!" She was blushing.

"What are you talking about? You're excited because I'm leaving on a night train?!"

"Oh no, Everett, my dear, I treasure our time. It's just that I'm so excited for you."

"What's this all about?"

"Manifesta is ready for your close-up, Everett!"

*   *   *

With Beatrice leading the way, Everett was ushered from the well-lighted LA Prime restaurant to a somber embarkation point, one with a broad carpeted stairwell leading downward. There was a pair of chairs flanking the stairwell landing and a signpost in an upright frame. The sign read "The BonaVista" in big gold letters, followed by the description, "Revolving Cocktail Lounge" and a long golden arrow pointing downward, indicating that the revolving lounge with a good view was currently revolving somewhere beneath their feet, spinning slowly and continuously—rotating in the manner of an old-fashioned LP record.

Beatrice paused just before she and Everett descended the carpeted steps together. She asked him a leading question: "Do you happen to know what the Fabulous Manifesta even looks like?"

"No, I've never seen her in person, nor in print. I only know what the tabloids say," he quipped.

"And what, might I ask, do the tabloids say?"

"I'd rather not repeat it," he answered.

"Oh, come now, Everett, you can tell me; I'm a full-fledged cosmopolitan girl," the heiress said imploringly, taking his arm and drawing him closer as they walked down the steps.

"The Hollywood tabloids claim that the fabulous and reclusive Manifesta is—and I quote—the most beautiful lesbian in the world. There, are you happy now?"

"I know that, silly. I just wanted to hear you say it." She giggled.

The BonaVista Cocktail Lounge was dimly lit in a shadowy, low-key fashion, emphasizing the kaleidoscopic treasure trove of LA city lights gleaming in from window after window: from looming hulks of surrounding skyscrapers, to necklaces of pixelated traffic lights streaming ceaselessly in the metropolis, to the pearl-like strings of streetlamps outlining the Hollywood Hills, and beyond that, the far-reaching diaphanous curtain of haze and glow that defines and delimits the Los Angeles Basin at night.

From where Everett stood, safe and warm, wined and dined, and in very good company, everything outside the grand floor-to-ceiling windows appeared to be moving too remotely in a world that was revolving entirely beyond his reach, a world, he shuddered to think, that may no longer even exist for him. He searched the lounge. His eyes adjusted to the low-key lighting.

Everett could make out the basic accoutrements of a Hollywood filmmaking setup: large HMI mercury arc lamps, movie cameras, dollies, riggings, and video monitors. He could tell that the electrical feeds were presently active by the gleam of the LEDs, which stood out like tiny holiday lights on the otherwise unlit set. Among the arrays of cameras and lights, he saw a glint from what appeared to be propellers or fan blades forming the backdrop for a makeshift thrust stage. He could recognize the components of a public address sound system scaled for a live cafe performance: the amplifiers, sound mixers, signal processing equalizers, tall power speakers, low monitor speakers, and microphones set on stands, all standing empty in the dark. The BonaVista Lounge was otherwise empty; there was no one else in the slowly revolving lounge to be seen, only an anonymous audience, with the aforementioned exterior illumination reaching the interior. The movie set with its thrust stage stood empty. A congregation of lounge chairs, standing expectantly in pairs, stood empty beside bistro tables whose solemn unlit candles bore witness.

Without any warning, Beatrice boldly ushered Everett into the stagelike setting with the gracefulness of an accomplished ballroom dancer taking the lead. Before Everett could object or withdraw, the gossamer heiress drew him close to her lovely feminine frame as she whispered seductively into his ear, "Make a wish for a finer time, handsome." She seemed to be imploring him. They danced together without music in an intimate fashion. "And hold fast to that thought," she prompted, before releasing Everett onstage, who was equally aroused and bewildered.

There was no announcement over the PA system, no countdown to zero for this Beatrice and Manifesta dog and pony show. There was no overture. All at once, the stage lights began arcing and flooding and spotting. The curious array of propellers began spinning faster. The movie cameras began recording and capturing action; the projectors began projecting light; and the loudspeakers screeched to life with the unmistakable romping-stomping sounds of Ambrosia Parsley from Reseda belting out "Skin and Bone" from her *Weeping*

Cherry album, singing with the femme fatale retro-contemporary confidence of a Roaring Twenties cabaret singer.

With minimalist percussion and a pounding piano beat, Ambrosia's vocals at once grabbed and taunted the listener: "Hey, mystery, come paint my face," the sexy girlish cabaret singer sang over the professional sound system. "No laughing, no dancing; just look at this place! You can have all the butterflies back, just please leave him alone!"

A rising chorus sang out, "La-la-la-la-la," providing sublime emotional emphasis.

Everett wheeled around to a dizzying guitar lick, while the stage lights, cameras, and virtual projections continued to flash and pop, to record and project, all at the same time, making it impossible for him to see or make out anything but startling flashes and fading afterimages.

Suddenly, a shimmering mirage appeared and developed into the image of a woman wearing a sexy sleeveless low-cut tomato-red halter dress. It was astonishing, right before his eyes.

Directly behind this emergent female figure, there appeared another mirage. Slowly, the specter of a tall, bearded gentleman wearing a black tuxedo began to materialize. After this well-dressed gentleman had materialized, he inexplicably approached the woman, who seemed to be Asian, from behind—and he blindfolded her with the theatrical flair of a masquerade, using a provocative bright red sash to cover her eyes.

The tuxedo-wearing man literally vanished into thin air, whereas the masqueraded avatar, the Asian female beauty, remained present, her long black hair erotically plaited and flowing down upon her breast, her exquisite feminine form held in that low-cut form-fitting tomato-red silk dress. Then her evocative figure came even more sharply into focus, hovering eerily before the speechless poet with the relative brilliance and high-resolution hyperreality of a virtual 3D holographic display.

The entire lounge was resonating with reverbed guitar and pounding percussion when the female soloist's voice declared with lamentation and stunning finality: "I'll take the great unknown. All the beauty's been blown from the sky, from the sea, from the sand!"

Even so, the percussive beat continued on without ceasing, beyond the final utterance of the post-Beat lyrics. And with each successive musical repetition, the image of the provocative, still-blindfolded Asian beauty in the revealing tomato-red halter dress grew larger than life, and then larger than that, and then even larger. And then the music ended abruptly. The thrust stage went dark, and the larger-than-life image of the female beauty simply vanished, leaving only a faint scent of ozone remaining in the slowly revolving cocktail lounge.

Waltzed around, spun out, and left bewildered, Everett looked to Beatrice for guidance.

"So, when do I get to meet the Fabulous Manifesta in person?"

"That's it, Everett. I'm sure Manifesta and her team can take it from here. I'm sure she has everything she needs, superficially, that is. Consider yourself captured." She giggled again.

"So, we're done here, are we?"

"No, we are not nearly finished. Everett. The best is surely yet to come. And it surely includes the Big Sur wilderness. But we do need to hurry now! We must get you to the Angels Flight Railway station pronto!" she said, beginning to usher Everett hurriedly back up the carpeted stairs.

"Hey! What about my luggage?" he protested, as she rushed with him to the elevator.

"Everything will be provided, Everett," Beatrice assured him without explaining.

"But—"

"You must go quickly now to the California Plaza, where I have a private investigator with human resources waiting."

"But—"

"It's only a few blocks from here, and I assume you know the way. But you must hurry now!" She ushered Everett to the elevator door, adding the following personalized instructions: "The Clovis point has been made! On Sunset Boulevard, of all places! Remember the phrase, Everett. It will serve as both a password and a passport!"

Chapter 2

The doors of the glass elevator pod closed, and Everett found himself alone, high up and out on a limb, that is, a ledge atop the Los Angeles Bonaventure Hotel. He felt the sudden free falling, an impromptu letting go amid the emptiness, the nothingness, and the LA glittery glow surrounding him, and yet he felt strangely secure. There he stood, tenuously suspended by unseen threads, balancing flat-footed and empty-handed on the polished floor of a glass elevator pod that had been electromechanically jettisoned off the proverbial ledge thirty-five floors up. And now he was free-falling, in the dead of night, into the foreboding darkness of downtown Los Angeles, free-falling with the slow, relentless, unstoppable downward drift of a reluctant parachute jumper dropped behind enemy lines—perhaps a Screaming Eagle free-falling into Carentan, France; or a paratrooper in training at Hightstown, New Jersey; or a civilian parachutist descending without hazard or discomfort at the World's Fair in Flushing Meadows, New York; or a summer vacationer bailing out over the blistering beaches of Coney Island. Or maybe it was the Sky Jump parachute ride that used to operate at Knott's Berry Farm in Buena Park, California.

Everett couldn't recall where or when as the elevator pod slid silently through the angular glass ceiling of the postmodern hotel. He crash-landed into a realistic model of a rocky tidal beach. The tidal beach extended ankle-deep into the reflecting pools of an architectural lagoon, where the downward plunging of the elevator pod abruptly stopped. The elevator doors opened, and Everett stepped out into the variegated lighting of the soaring and disorienting hotel lobby.

He made his way through a dizzying series of spotlighted reflecting pools with spouting water fountains, hanging gardens, and curvilinear partitions. It was a rarified and self-contained world, which took on a somber tone in the late evening hours, as did the pairs of oval observation seating pods peering down from a great height—each pair like the enormous spectacles of Doctor T. J. Eckleburg, the storied optometrist who may or may not have been in the business of oversight any longer.

Everett remembered from his down-and-out time on the LA streets that there remained a historic network of elevated pedestrian walkways, or pedways, connecting the downtown financial district to Bunker Hill, where he found himself heading now in a hurry. Apparently, the concept of elevated pedways built on raised bridges and pedestrian corridors placed high above the endlessly streaming freeway traffic was only the initial phase of a futuristic utopian LA city plan, a plan that was to be followed by the construction of an elevated stratum of mechanized people-moving escalators, monorails, and trams, all operating in accordance with the boldly idealistic, if somewhat quixotic, Disneyesque and now defunct vision of the city planners, who had elevated the status of *the individual*, in theory, to portable pedestrian wayfarer—elevated the status of the individual in terms of mobility, prominence, safety, purview, and access to the public events and cultural venues of downtown Los Angeles—by providing sky bridges well above the bedlam, as opposed to rudely herding human beings, in threatening juxtaposition to one another, into the constant commotion, noise pollution, gridlock, and dangers of the unrelenting freeway traffic streaming below.

Everett knew that the antiquated pedways in question were accessed well above street level. Therefore, rather than head directly out through the main exit of the hotel lobby, he turned and hurried back up a spiral staircase, and then went up another flight, and then another, in search of telltale signage. He climbed to the level of a dimly lit gymnasium encircled by an indoor running track, where sporadic clutches of anonymous hotel guests, occupied with personal exercise equipment, appeared oblivious to his plight. It was in the process of climbing the stairs that Everett's body reminded him that he was no longer as nimble as he used to be, before he was desperately, imprudently dunked, drowned, pounded, and dragged, then washed up on the beach. There was no doubt about it: he knew exactly when it happened. Back then, he had acquired a rather unfortunate and nearly incurable physical condition that is recognized in the medical literature as a limp.

Circling the hotel atrium running track with a painful hitch in his step, hurriedly searching the architectural colonnade for a way to exit the iconic building via the old bone remnants of the utopian pedestrian skyway, Everett spied a signpost with an arrow pointing to yet another cylindrical column with yet another set of spiraling stairs, leading him up to the rarefied pedway that was still in the business of ferrying urban pedestrians over South Flower Street.

Bursting out from the hotel into a dense, dripping layer of mist and maritime fog, Everett zipped his leather jacket up to his neckline before he headed out on the lesser-traveled span of the rain-drenched pedway, which was ill-illumined and empty. He saw that his way ahead was lighted only sporadically by the few foot lamps that were still working.

Midway across the long, broad, plank-like walkway in the sky, Everett turned back around without stopping his progress to gaze up at the impressive bronzed glass towers of the Bonaventure Hotel he had just exited. Walking backward while looking up, he watched the tiny external gondolas kinetically ascending and descending from the brink of what appeared to the washed-up, spun-out emo songwriter to be one colossal quatrefoil fountain, and the words of Longfellow's epic poem "Evangeline," penned circa 1847, came upon him: "That which the fountain sends forth returns again to the fountain." He sounded the words, so familiar in his mind, and yet in the depths of his own broken heart, he could still hear the funeral dirge of Evangeline's sad ocean and could still feel the weight of his own lost love as his poor soul wandered in want and cheerless discomfort, bleeding, barefooted, walking over the shards and thorns of his existence. While stumbling backward and looking upward, he reflectively mused.

Everett turned around again and quickened his pace to reach the end of the pedestrian sky bridge, where it opened out on a parklike promenade with raised gardens and public pop art sculptures affectionately referred to as "plop art" in this part of town. Without any direct lighting, the naked *Handstand Boy*, cast in bronze, took on the sinister appearance of a giant spider hanging upside down from a diaphanous tree. Likewise, the inverted female gymnast, suspended in time and unnaturally arched upside down on a balance beam, looked precarious. The stunning bronze and stainless steel casting entitled *Alchemy of the Human Spirit* issued forth with an uncanny spectral gleam, the high-polished chrome of the gymnast's contrasting leotard sublimely reflecting the LA night-lights. To Everett's right, the low geometric hulk of the Ketchum Downtown YMCA building loomed dark and empty as he strode hurriedly by, its contiguous walls of windows, once filled with images of health and vitality, appearing to him bleak, threatening, and mirrorlike as a result of the building's being largely unlit from within.

The concrete plaza was completely unlit, as if some prankster had turned off all the electricity. The resulting mood was more than that brought about by dank misty rain and mere gloominess; it was a mood of dread. The dreadfulness was accented by the absence of anyone walking anywhere within Everett's sight. It was as if he, the lone pedestrian wayfarer, were entering a ghost town. *But this is no ghost town,* he reminded himself. *This is downtown Los Angeles post-Y2K, for heaven's sake!*

Everett managed to regain his bearings at the sight of three familiar female figures standing at the spot where Fourth Street ramped up to meet with the Ketchum YMCA's promenade at the corner of Fourth and Hope. Alas, not a one of these lovely women was either moving or breathing this evening. Known affectionately as the "the Three Graces," personifying beauty, charm, and joy, each of these lovely women had been chiseled out of solid limestone long ago. Everett hurried across the empty intersection to the redbrick pavement of a giant bank and then to the narrow sidewalk on Fourth Street. *Just one more city block now,* he thought. Just one more block to reach the California Plaza for his departure on some kind of private sojourn that had been scheduled for him by Miss Beatrice, a private sojourn that ostensibly was to begin at the uppermost station of the Angels Flight funicular railway.

Shivers crept up Everett's spine when he saw the flames in barrels and the first of many homeless tents crowding the sidewalks of a broad underpass that ran beneath Grand Avenue and the financial district skyscrapers of Bunker Hill. Everett paused. Instinctively, he wanted to fade into the protective cloak of darkness and not move an inch until he had adequately scoped out the situation for any danger, but he was in a hurry. He steeled himself and advanced directly into the homeless tent village as he had often done back then.

There comes a time when the bright candy-apple gloss of human desire and ambition gives way to the concrete tongue of a darker city, the rough grating tongue of a harder, harsher reality: one that skins the knees, and tears the flesh, and breaks the bones as it brings both waif and wayfarer to their knees or, worse, to the brink of life and death. Everett knew too well the dangers of one: *Just one more unfortunate roadkill for this stone-cold sepulcher by the sea. Nada mas!* he reminded himself.

Everett pressed forward on what little sidewalk remained unoccupied, respectfully nodding a polite howdy-do as he passed by the tents and curious cowering inhabitants, hoping against hope that he would make it through this dreadful gauntlet of subhuman habitation without being accosted. He could feel the penetrating eyes of the faceless residents watching him from the shadows as he moved closer to the flaming trash barrels, hoping to squeeze on through rather than cut and run and head back the same way he had come. The well-traveled vagabond had learned on the streets how and when to meet and hold a strong man's gaze, each acknowledging their common humanity, and when to scrap his own agenda in a romantic, if not heroic, effort to fulfill a vaguely defined mission that he, among others, considered to be more valuable than either silver or gold.

Approaching the relative brightness of a row of three trash cans, each in flames, Everett's night vision adjusted to the glare in his immediate foreground. Suddenly, he encountered a large, formidable homeless dude purposefully blocking his way.

"You can't go any farther!" said the homeless dude, speaking in a proper declarative sentence.

"Well, that's precisely where I'm heading!" Everett responded in kind, meeting and holding his opponent's challenging gaze in the flickering firelight.

Everett could hear the zipping sounds and many tent flaps opening. He could hear the shuffling sounds of feet moving on concrete and could sense a crowd gathering around him. Even in the darkness, he could feel the penetrating eyes of all the crepuscular creatures.

"I'm warning you again! You can't go any farther!" the lead homeless dude said, repeating himself, while flashing Everett an outstretched palm as a predetermined gesture.

"And I'm reminding you nicely: that's precisely where I'm heading, dude!"

Just when things appeared to be on the brink of escalating and getting out of hand, the lead homeless dude offered up a modicum of explanation: "There is a certified badass up yonder wreaking havoc!" he exclaimed. "That badass just threw poor Brandon down a flight of stairs. You tell him, Brandon," he insisted, pointing to a shadowy figure lying on the sidewalk.

The gathered crowd parted. Brandon, who was lying sideways, curled up on his cardboard mattress beneath an unzipped alpine sleeping bag, moaning briefly as he repositioned himself, struggled to comply. "He threw me down a flight of steps—that's what he did," he explained. "For no good reason."

"See, I told you so. You can't go there! Brandon is all beat up. From the looks of him, that badass in the snap-brim fedora must have bounced him down every blessed step on Bunker Hill."

Everett, quickly surmising the situation, thanked the lead homeless dude and Brandon kindly for their concern and their consideration for his physical well-being. "However," he added, "might I be so bold as to ask why this certified badass in the snap-brim fedora would bounce poor Brandon down those many flights of concrete steps of yonder Bunker Hill?"

"I have no clue," the lead homeless dude replied.

"What about you, Brandon?" Everett asked. "Do you have any clue as to why you got thrown down so hard and so harshly?"

Brandon shifted his position on the cardboard mat and removed his coverlet, revealing the evidence: many painful bruises. "The big bad man said something about a password, then he threw me down. He said I didn't have the right one!"

"I guess Brandon didn't have the right password," the lead homeless dude said.

The cordiality of the discourse encouraged the homeless crowd to move in closer to the fireside scene. "Hey! I know you!" a voice cried out in the darkness.

"Hey! Yo! I remember you!" another cried out.

"We know who the hell you are!" the crowd shouted out simultaneously.

"I'm not that guy anymore!" exclaimed Everett. The homeless crowd murmured.

"You're Everett Durant!" came forth a voice in an accusatory tone.

"Hey, Everett," an anonymous voice said, cackling loudly, "whatever happened to the beauty?!"

Everett was unfazed by the taunts of the accusatory crowd; he had heard it all before. And now, with the issue of time pressing in upon him and with a night train to catch, he prepared an expedient exit strategy: "All I can tell you about the beauty." He paused, rubbing the palms of his hands together before the flames as if to both warm his hands and mystify the crowd.

"All I can tell you about the beauty that you fine folks here don't already know …" The orator paused again, heightening the suspense, shifting his position in relation to the assembly, and waxing theatrical, as if he needed to look more deeply into the flames of the fire to summon just the right words of explanation. "All I can tell you about the beauty that you folks don't already know," he repeated, looking out into a sea of dark tents and the shadows teeming with homeless eyes. "Alas, all I can tell you about the beauty is that beauty is fleeting—fleeting like you!" Everett emphasized the point with a slow, level sweep of his outstretched index finger across the assembly. "Fleeting like me!" he assured them all personally. "And I for one desperately wanna, am gonna, gotta go now!" Everett concluded his impromptu philosophical discourse with a climactic tragicomic stage bow.

With that humble gesture, Everett slipped unobstructed between two flaming municipal trash cans and immediately shifted his stride to a painful jogging pace, which he maintained until he reached the upper level of the sprawling California Plaza.

Located at the base of two giant mirrored skyscrapers on the pinnacle of Bunker Hill, the massive reinforced concrete platforms of the California Plaza created a soaring public event space with a dynamic water fountain, a performing arts amphitheater with open-air seating, and the uppermost terminal of the Angels Flight Railway station.

Everett paused at the steps of the amphitheater stage, where he was met by a flood of memories from another time in his life: memories of free-form concerts and hot summer nights; memories of touring with lesser-known groups; memories of live music outdoors under the stars, right here, with wall-to-wall people of all stripes, their tribal tattoos bobbing as they danced to the rhythm of the amplified alternative music in the jam-packed open-air plaza, with nobody standing still. But that was then, and this was now—a somber night where everything seemed to be clouded over with a gauzy shroud of dread, creating an even darker impression of the surrounding city.

Everett mounted the final steps to the Angels Flight Railway station with a high level of caution, considering what had happened to poor Brandon. He realized that everything once familiar to him had changed, and certainly not for the better. He knew that Charity Street had been renamed Grand Avenue by the Los Angeles City Council a long time ago and that the original name for what is now called Broadway Boulevard was once tagged with the appellation Calle de la Eternidad. Moreover, as a professor of post-Beat poetry, Everett recalled the vaporous lines of the prose poem "Aquí" or "Here" by Octavio Paz, vaporous lines and eerie mystical words that were memorialized, once upon a time, by their incorporation into a large colorful mural on a nearby Broadway facade. It was urban art depicting pre-Columbian figures amid an Aztec calendar motif, projecting figures with giant upward-reaching arms expressing acute feelings of exile and dislocation while making a soaring appeal to heaven.

As Everett cautiously mounted the concrete steps to the train station, he translated the Nobel laureate's poem "Aquí" from the original Spanish into English:

Here

My footsteps in this street

   resound

      in another street,

         where

            I hear my steps passing along another street,

               where

                  only the mist is real.

Chapter 3

Everett scoped out the nostalgic *mise-en-scène* as he approached the Beaux-Arts train station. The upper terminal of the Angels Flight Railway was enveloped in shadows. The surrounding metropolis was overcast and drenched in an inky hue. The bright orange pillars and black-trimmed spires of the ornate old-school station house were vaguely lit this time of night with the dull amber light of vintage incandescent bulbs, which only served to accentuate or obscure the obliqueness of the lines, the distorted shapes, and the unclear intentions of any mysterious characters who might be standing there in the darkness, hidden among the shadows.

Everett searched for forms in the shadows. He saw a hard-core official-looking man wearing what could only be described as an old-fashioned private investigator's trench coat and a classic snap-brim fedora. The man was holding a conspicuous black box leather attaché in his right hand, and with his left hand, which was in his coat pocket, he appeared to be handling a weapon of some sort. Perhaps it was a loaded handgun. *What is that password?* Everett thought as he strode into the claustrophobic causeway of the Angels Flight station.

Everett froze momentarily in midstride. He struggled to remember the exact phrasing of the password he had been given. In his confusion, he realized that he no longer had his wallet or his cell phone with him, his having left everything but the clothes he was wearing behind. The longer he stood pondering, the less he understood the meaning of the curious Clovis point. Finally, he retrieved the exact wording from his short-term memory: *The Clovis point has been made! On Sunset Boulevard, of all places!* Everett recalled the gossamer heiress speaking these words to him explicitly before they parted ways.

However, before Everett could offer up his spoken version of the aforementioned password, with the enigmatic Clovis point in mind, a second figure appeared abruptly. It was a strikingly beautiful blonde bombshell of a woman with shapely legs to boot. She was extremely attractive and alluring, a femme fatale, a potentially dangerous female, projecting a severe executive-like persona and dressed in tasteful conservative vintage business attire: a basic black and tan suit with a pencil skirt, white gloves, and a matching camel-colored snap-brim fedora.

The mysterious femme fatale / dangerous attractive businesswoman stepped out from behind the intimidating PI character, and as she did so, she held a small sign directly in front of her torso, like a limo driver waiting for a customer at the Los Angeles airport's baggage claim.

The meaning of the sign was clear enough to Everett Durant. Even in the shadows, with distorted lines and shapes, never mind the unclear intentions of the people facing him down in this tense situation, he immediately knew the meaning of the semiotics at hand. The sign bore the image of a treble clef, a typical feature of graphic design placed on a musical staff, indicating pitch, the clef curved, with the musical note G4 positioned on the staff above middle C—the G clef.

Everett walked forward with a renewed sense of confidence to face the music, as it were.

"You look like a deer in the headlights, Everett Durant," the intimidating tough-guy PI announced, eyeballing the tragic poet from topknot to toe tag. "It's no wonder Miss Beatrice contacted the Detective Dash Brogan Institute and sent for us to hold your hand!"

As he spoke, the PI slowly removed his left hand from his trench coat pocket while repeatedly pointing to his own broad chest with an extended thumb. "I'm Trenton Dostoyevsky, PI, for your information. And this here is Henrietta Haddonfield, from the HR department. She was sent along to babysit the untamed beast in me," he said with a smirk.

"Greetings, Everett," the shadowy woman said. Ignoring her colleague, she dropped the sign and stepped forward to greet the tragic poet with a surprisingly firm handshake.

"Actually, I was sent along to monitor and record the upcoming epic events and to mitigate the brutish, hard-boiled aspects of this troublesome business," she said, pointing her slender, white-gloved finger directly at Trenton Dostoyevsky, PI.

"Be nice, Henrietta. The traveling tambourine man has just met us."

The blonde bombshell / femme fatale simply smiled back at the tough-guy PI, then raised the index finger of her white-gloved hand to her ruby-red lips, indicating silence.

Speaking to Everett, Trenton asserted, "She means there have been some issues with the Dash Brogan Institute of True Crime related to missing persons, petrified children, and the appropriateness of so-called old-school police procedures in these here postmodern times."

"I mean what I mean, and that's what I mean," Henrietta announced somewhat sarcastically.

Everett shuffled nervously on the platform as he peered down the dimly lit archway spanning the steepest train tracks imaginable. There was a single orange railcar with black trim standing at a nearly impossible downward angle, apparently waiting for him. Intently following the narrow-gauge rails and their metallic shine with his eyes, he traced the line of the tracks all the way down to the bottom of the slope at Hill Street, where they seemed to disappear into a large, gaping hole in the pavement from which no discernible light escaped. The lower station at Hill Street with its disturbed and confused streetscape appeared to Everett to be one gigantic construction site defined by sawhorse barricades, caution signs, and steel perimeter fencing surrounded by reflective traffic cones that gave the giant cavernous hole in the pavement the ghastly, unnerving appearance of a great white shark approaching from the depths.

"Miss Beatrice said something about a password that I was supposed to remember, but she failed to mention I would be crash-landing into an unfinished construction site that looks like it's in ruins."

"I wouldn't be much of a private investigator if I needed a password to identify the rube in Carnytown now, would I, Everett Durant?"

"I guess not," Everett admitted. "So, what's it all about, Alfie? It looks like a short trip to Nowheresville from here. There's nothing but a huge construction site down below."

"Welcome to LA, Mister Tambourine Man, where huge unfinished construction sites are not that uncommon. Now that you're finally here, are you sure you're ready to take full responsibility?!" Trenton Dostoyevsky motioned to Everett, lifting his arm with the black box leather attaché extended.

"Ah, you brought me new luggage. How nice of you," Everett joked. "How can I ever thank you? I hazard to even guess."

"Funny guy for a washed-up tambourine man. Make a note, Henrietta, that the clueless rube starts out by laughing at us and talking nervous nonsense at the top of the drop."

"Rube, he says. A clueless rube, he calls me. Is that how the so-called Dash Brogan Institute of True Crime treats its valued customers?"

"Miss Beatrice is the paying customer, Tambourine Man. You are … you are—" He paused. "What is he listed as technically, Henrietta?"

"Technically, he is listed on the ledger as Everett Durant, a VIP instrument of conveyance."

"Well then, let's get on with it! I'm getting tired of carrying this preposterous attaché."

The attaché that Trenton Dostoevsky had held out for inspection would have been easily recognized by cognoscenti of luxury goods as an authentic *sac à depeche* black box calf leather briefcase made by Hermès of Paris, one of the most famous, most exclusive, and most coveted items of the whole distinguished collection. This particular Hermès *sac à depeche* attaché featured a double-lock closure, which was extremely rare. The elegant, doubly secured model had long been a favorite of aristocrats, royals, heads of state, and the international jet set. The palladium-plated hardware—considered to be even more rare than gold or platinum—shone out amid the vague shadows and reflections of the Angels Flight station lights with a lustrous silvery-white sheen.

"Which hand do you want to use, right or left?!" Trenton Dostoevsky barked, holding the Hermès attaché up again for visual inspection. As he spoke, the impatient PI reached back into his trench coat pocket and withdrew a pair of metal handcuffs connected by a linked chain. The man proceeded to clamp one handcuff to the handle of the *sac à depeche* as he continued barking: "I recommend you pick a hand you won't mind not using for quite a while. Not to scratch with, not to strum with, not even to shake a tambourine with!" He explained the procedure with a gesture, showing Everett the unclamped half of the handcuff with an unsettling grin.

"What the—" Everett shouted, backing away from the Hermès attaché.

"It's an official matter of chain of custody! You tell him, Henrietta," Trenton said, dropping the briefcase back to his side.

"He's right, Everett. Chain of custody refers to the documentation that serves as a record of the control, transfer, and disposition of evidence in an important criminal or medical case."

"Hold on now, the both of you!" Everett warned. He continued backing away from the handcuffs. "Miss Beatrice didn't mention that I would have to be handcuffed and hurled into a scary dark tunnel with no lights, with no road map and no purpose I can even begin to see."

"Miss Beatrice knows the rules, even if the clueless rube doesn't get it yet."

"There he goes again with the clueless rube talk. Is that supposed to engender confidence?"

Henrietta Haddonfield, HR, smiled with an assuring, alluringly feminine smile. "Miss Beatrice certainly knows what she is doing, Everett. And so do we! Verily, Everett, it is in the transition from one's current limited station, social position, and perspective to another, more favorable position, which is most difficult for some people to accomplish alone."

"There's that!" Trenton smirked. "Plus, Miss Beatrice assured us that you are our guy."

"And just what kind of *guy* is that?" Everett demanded. Feeling a mixture of curiosity and resolve, he cautiously approached the shady couple.

Henrietta Haddonfield thumbed through the pages of her official-looking ledger and paused at a particular page. "Miss Beatrice informed us expressly, and I quote, 'Everett Durant is a tragic guy who won't bolt when things get scary.'"

Everett replied, "That's not terribly reassuring, Miss Henrietta Haddonfield from the HR department. And you, Mister Hard-Boiled He-Man, what did Miss Beatrice tell you about me?"

"She told me that Everett Durant could carry a tune. That's all I needed to know, big shot!" Trenton growled, "Now step right up, Mister Tambourine Man! Pick a hand! Either hand! I'll hook you up properly while Henrietta here does the formalities. Now, let's get a move on! We've got a deadly serious night train to catch!"

There was loud metallic *click* as the handcuff was firmly clamped onto Everett's left wrist.

The unexpected weight of the Hermès black box leather briefcase caused Everett's left shoulder to slump. It took him a few moments to recover, straining and staggering, attempting to walk upright and appear nonchalant, once he'd been handed the burdensome attaché.

After the handcuffing, and after Henrietta had completed the official documents, Trenton Dostoyevsky entered the station house, where the programmable logic controller, a computer system, was housed.

The hard-boiled PI returned from the station house with a long slender tree branch in his hand. After opening the narrow gate that led to the railcar's declivitous loading platform, he shouted with a train conductor's élan, "All aboard!"

Henrietta Haddonfield was the first to enter the iconic railcar, followed by Everett Durant, who moved gingerly down the narrow-stepped aisle, reaching from vertical pole to vertical pole, grasping each one, using his free hand for support. Henrietta swung her shadowy self into a side-facing passenger seat. She smiled up at Everett as he passed by, working his way down the steep steps to the front of the downward-facing railcar.

Everett, still standing in the aisle, turned around and saw Trenton Dostoyevsky, PI, reaching back awkwardly toward the unoccupied station house. He was brandishing the tree branch like Aaron brandishing his rod, his arm outstretched in an effort to reach, then push, the computer's start button.

"Way down we go, Kaleo!" Trenton shouted with élan, as the brake was released and the railcar began to descend into the unknown with a massive gathering rush of potential energy.

Everett swung back around to peer down at the tracks through the archway. Seeing a frightening unfinished construction site looming dead ahead, he braced himself for a major head-on collision and a crash-landing into the fast-approaching hollows of the structural deconstruction. *Hast thou eyes of flesh!?* he thought frantically. *Do you see as a modern man sees!? Is any of this Angels Flight business even possible? Is any of this really happening? to me? to any of us? to each of us? to all of us? Yet again?*

As the rapidly descending railcar fell into the darkness, the metallic brakes engaged with a loud shrieking sound. As this was going on, the hollow, expanding construction zone with its arches and toothy barricades became a ghastly tunnel of screams.

The human eyes of flesh with their crystalline lenses and photoreceptive retinas can only process so much information themselves before shooting a live feed to the optic chiasmus and thus to the pineal gland, a discerning hub, and relaying the visual information to the sensory distribution center of the thalamus, which shines its neurological light onto the occipital cortex, that is, a cinematic multiplex located near the back of the skull—but not before sending a somewhat reliable feed to the two horns of the hypothalamus, where would-be memories are recorded, preserved, and consolidated, and ultimately to the limbic system's amygdaloid complex, where strong emotions including fear are processed.

Suddenly, Everett, feeling the full weight of the Hermès attaché he was carrying through this tunnel of screams, entered a state of high anxiety—albeit a state of high anxiety with his admittedly fragile, yet equally resilient and determined, ego firmly in place. Again and again, Everett heard the shrieking screams of the brakes attempting to slow the perilous descent of the railcar. He knew they were not his screams. That made it even worse.

It is well-known that intense anxiety can cause visual hallucinations, including tunnel vision, distortion of geometric shapes and proportions, and colorful flashes of light. Indeed, hyperconnectivity between the amygdala (where emotion and meaning are mingled with memories) and the visual cortex (serving higher-order visual functions) is often related to seizures brought on by distressing, if not thoroughly incapacitating, visual hallucinations.

Everett fell headlong into the inky neonoir of the nostalgic *mise-en-scène* at an oblique angle. It was as though he were entering the long, hollow chamber of a medical scanning device, one with positron emission scanning and computed tomography—for a fractured bone perhaps, or a dreaded cancer diagnosis, or to find the cause of madness or dementia. But this long, hollow chamber was so much longer, so much louder, and so much larger than any of those devices. He felt a twinge. A black pool opened at his feet. He dived in. It had no bottom.

*   *   *

Everett slowly regained a torpid sort of consciousness, which allowed him to perceive a loud roaring and rumbling sensorium around him, but not enough to enable him to react to it. This sensorium was punctuated by a constant tapping rhythm he could recognize: it had the tempo of a locomotive moving fast on steel tracks, the beats defined as the metallic wheels skimmed and bumped over the more uneven expansion joints in passing. Everett could hear human voices very close to him, but he was unable to move, much less respond, or even cry out. He was content to lie still in a dreamlike state of paralysis and listen intently in the darkness, lying motionlessly with a rising feeling of suspense, lest there be danger.

"Time for us to send the official dispatch to Miss Beatrice, Henrietta." That gruff voice: it was the hard-boiled, whiskey- and tobacco-soaked voice of Trenton Dostoyevsky, PI, speaking over the roaring of the speeding locomotive.

"How exactly would you like me to word the official dispatch?" Everett heard the alluring and reassuring voice of Henrietta Haddonfield, HR, respond agreeably.

"Tell her the *Fram* has sailed. She'll get it!" Trenton barked loudly, adding a laugh.

Listening while inert, Everett overheard Henrietta responding in a familiar way: "Anything else, dear?"

"Tell her that the lords-a-leaping are none too pleased," Trenton Dostoyevsky added.

"I'll send the dispatch right away, Trent. But seriously, what do you mean by that?"

"It appears the lords-a-leaping tried to latch on again during the LA transit. Like a wart on a toe or a recurring pimple on a butt. We appear to have acquired a not-so-secretive caboose!"

"Do you think they might be the intellectual property *Pirates of the Caribbean*, or the criminal lawyers of the Cayman Islands, or the wrought iron gatekeepers and lobbyists of Gaithersburg who have managed to gain a stranglehold on the priorities and conduct of the life sciences in our lifetime, not to mention the stifling of alternative medicaments and vital human resources?"

"One or more of the above, Henrietta. But it's not our problem! At least not mine! You know as well as I do that the Dash Brogan Institute of True Crime is explicit on the matter of people with devious intentions and/ or squishy loyalties. No mixed loyalties—that's pretty clear. Check and see if it isn't mentioned somewhere in your ledger."

"So, what do you intend to do, Trenton?"

"What I always do: handle it! I'll handle it like old Detective Dash Brogan himself!"

"Can you at least try to handle it humanely, dear?"

"I can do better than that. I can handle it with the delicacy of a person executing poetic justice."

"I assume you're going to execute the Edgar Allan Poe severance gambit once again?"

"Yes, my little chickadee. I'm gonna forever dissever this speeding locomotive from one covetous caboose that carries the envy of disgruntled angels and demons down under the sea."

"Do be careful, Trenton."

The sounds of distant whistles and bells came and went; an occasional air horn sounded; rails squealed under the strain of a massive speeding locomotive going around a curve. The rhythmic rhapsody and soothing monotony of the train wheels rolling effortlessly along the unseen tracks caused Everett to drift off, once again, into a deep, bottomless sleep.

*   *   *

Everett rose to wakefulness feeling like *the* passenger that Iggy Pop sang about, the one who rides and rides through the city's darker underside at night—the passenger who stays under glass, as on a speeding train, as he rides and rides under a dark and hollow sky along a winding ocean drive through a blighted hollow city at night, singing, "La-la-la-la-la-la-la-la, la-la-la-la-la-la-la-la, la-la-la-la-la-la-la-la, la-la-la." The familiar chorus faded back to become part of his distant protopunk garage band memories again. As Everett awakened, he found that he was indeed chained to a very real and relatively heavy Hermès *sac à depeche* attaché. Thus, he arose not only to wakefulness but also with a compelling sense of mystery and commotion, yet with little, if any, knowledge about what this attaché held or how it was related to this VIP method of conveyance.

"Ahoy! Henrietta! The sleeping songbird rises, looking a tad worse for wear."

"Ah. So, it wasn't all a dream after all." Everett opened his eyes as he spoke in bewilderment. "This chain. This Hermès attaché. This moving train car—"

"Welcome to America, Rip Van Winkle. Don't worry, we won't start the next cultural revolution without you," Trenton Dostoyevsky, PI, remarked, clicking on a dim lamp.

"So, where are we? Did we crash? How is it we are still moving?!" Everett demanded.

"Welcome to the underground railroad, Everett!" Trenton Dostoyevsky barked.

"I recall I heard voices, your voices. Trenton, you were saying something about severing an unwanted caboose. And you, Henrietta, were saying something about *Pirates of the Caribbean*."

"Comatose can be like that," Trenton gibed. "Rest now, and gather your wits."

Everett looked over to Henrietta Haddonfield. She was sitting directly across from him, seated comfortably in an upholstered velvet chair in what appeared to be the high-end drawing room of a luxurious parlor/ sleeping car commissioned from the Pullman Palace Car Company during the Gilded Age. Inspecting the decor, Everett noticed that the floor of the luxurious Pullman parlor car was covered with a deep-red Persian carpet; the walls were covered in polished panels of rich mahogany, beveled mirrors, polished brass fittings, and handcrafted cabinets; the arched and paneled ceilings supported rows of skylights and a lineup of unlit crystal chandeliers; and the black glass windows were framed by velvet curtains hanging in heavy folds. Henrietta Haddonfield looked up from her ledger and smiled, unperturbed.

"I remember a dark and scary tunnel," Everett exclaimed. He sat upright. "And I heard such terrible screams. Even now, everything appears to me way too dark and scary, including this speeding locomotive and this poorly illuminated train car." He looked around while reclining awkwardly on a tufted velvet bench. "Check out these windows, folks. It looks to me like all these windows have been painted over with stage paint or something else that is lurid, dark, and nasty."

"There's a reason for that! Which you might have missed in your comatose state of mind."

"Well, I'm awake now. Can you tell me why these windows appear to be all painted black?"

"It looks that way because it's nighttime, Everett. It looks dark outside because it's overcast and there is no poetic moon this evening to shine like a ghostly galleon tossed upon cloudy seas. Things look pitch-black, Everett, because it's nearly three o'clock in the morning and we're on a night train in the middle of nowhere, hammering hard and fast before dawn draws nigh."

"Oh, that could be, now that you mention it," Everett admitted, feeling duly embarrassed. "I reckon the heightened drama of this evening might explain the stage paint I thought I saw," he mused. "You mean this late-night train ride is all totally film noir, like *Strangers on a Train*, the classic black-and-white movie? Seriously, Trenton, it feels to me like we're traveling into a classic Hollywood Hitchcock movie where mysterious, dubious dudes with ill intentions hatch their devious plans to commit murder in their private Pullman cars, or should I say royal cabooses?"

"There are no strangers on this train, Everett! Only impertinent observers pretending not to notice us!" Trenton Dostoyevsky barked, intending his outburst to serve as a warning to any would-be wise guys.

"Bear with me as I get my bearings," Everett said. He struggled to reposition the handcuffs, the chain, and the hefty Hermès attaché so they'd all feel more comfortable. "Can I assume that this night train and this underground railroad, as you call it, has something to do with Miss Beatrice?"

"Yes, Everett. This train and this underground railroad has everything to do with Miss Beatrice," Henrietta Haddonfield answered in a pleasing, professional, reassuring voice.

"So, what's with this curious 'the *Fram* has sailed' dispatch to Miss Beatrice? Or is this a special dispatch, an encrypted one that requires a special password?"

"Bright bard we have here, Henrietta. Proves Everett can carry a tune and remember a password at the same time. Imagine that! He might have a snowball's chance in hell for safe passage after all." Trenton Dostoyevsky was reclining as he spoke, with his snap-brim fedora pointing down, covering his face, and his feet up on a short bench next to Everett, who was sitting directly across from Henrietta's velvet-upholstered chair.

Each passenger was facing the interior of the shadowy palatial parlor car as it rumbled and rolled at top speed toward an unknown location in the middle of Nowheresville, USA. It was still far from the break of dawn, nearing the ghostly hour of three o'clock in the morning, when the veil between the wider world grows thin and the thought that anything can happen begins to emerge like an apparition in such a shadowy liminal zone as this.

"Miss Beatrice requested that our communications be encrypted," Henrietta explained, calmly turning the pages of her official ledger. "For purposes of client confidentiality, of course."

"So, you're saying I need to recite the password correctly like a trained monkey in order to receive a bright and colorful candy-coated gumball of an allegory as a reward? Is that it?"

"Close, but no cigar, Everett!" Trenton barked. "Try again on the big wheel, old sport."

"Look, folks, I don't mean to be rude or unappreciative of your awesome underground efforts, but what if I suddenly decide not to play along? I certainly don't know what's inside this fancy briefcase you've hooked me up to," he declared, holding up the formidable Hermès attaché. "How could I possibly be responsible for its dispensation or its conveyance?" Everett tested the tensile strength of the adamantine chain as he protested against his plight. "Look at this, would you? I'm a bagman for Miss Beatrice! What if I decide I want out of this frantically hurried VIP conveyance business—out of this mysterious cloak-and-dagger delivery boy business—entirely? What then?"

"We can't help you there, Mister Reluctant Tambourine Man!" Trenton barked. "You made your own decision to journey forth into Adventureland. We simply made the requisite chain of custody official for one highly specialized and highly coveted Hermès attaché."

"What if I suddenly decide I want out of this?" Everett said half-heartedly.

"There is no out," Henrietta Haddonfield, HR, explained.

"Then where's the key to these handcuffs? This chain looks impossibly strong to me!"

"There is no key," Henrietta said sympathetically.

"And so, exactly how does one escape the burdensome task of conveying this Hermès attaché with a seemingly unbreakable chain of custody and no key?"

Trenton Dostoyevsky, PI, sat up, pushed back his snap-brim fedora, and smiled darkly. "I might recommend an ax!" he quipped. Then he lay back down, laughing, and lowered the snap brim of his fedora over his face once again. "You tell him what he needs to know, Henrietta. He's carrying the Clovis point into the future, whether he realizes it yet or not. Meanwhile, I'm gonna try to catch a few good winks. You fill in the blanks for him."

Henrietta Haddonfield's Wild West tale began with a sigh of resignation, then she began telling Everett Durant the tale of the great historic showdown at the corner of Hollywood and Sunset Boulevards. "It was an epic heavyweight showdown that happened in three distinct phases or acts," she said, "that is, the throw-down, the beatdown, and the slap-down." She checked her ledger as she spoke.

"This all took place once upon a time in LA at the crossroads where Hollywood Boulevard, Hillhurst Avenue, Virgil Avenue, and Sunset Boulevard converge, creating a stage for the wider world to witness the players, the poseurs, the card sharks, the card cheats, the backstabbers, the outright frauds, the deceivers, the exploiters, the dandies, the proud idols, the superfluous, the obnoxious, and the idiotic. In other words, all the Great Big Phonies. 'Such persons are like the figures which are introduced in tragedies, for as they have the shape, and dress, and personal appearance of an actor, but are not actors, so also physicians are many in title but very few in reality' (excerpted from the law of Hippocrates, circa 400 BC)—not so different now from then, we see, as this Wild West tale of woe and redemption unfolds." She spoke with the self-assurance of a seasoned storyteller.

Everett cozied up to Henrietta and her Wild West tale, clutching the Hermès attaché with both hands and listening intently to her voice as the speeding locomotive roared into the dark of night.

"Whenever the world is seriously threatened with monstrous evil, chaos, or otherwise vile and destructive forces," she said, her tone soothing and melodious, "whenever a hapless, helpless individual all alone, or a village, or a culture, or an entire population of innocent and uninformed citizens, is left dangling on the chains of failed expectations or, worse, left dangling on the ropes of despair with no hope at all, an avenging angel of creativity is sent forth into the fray, right into the center of the gritty, blood-soaked boulevard, directly into the high drama of a veritable historical showdown—filmed and recorded for posterity in medias res!

"What started off well enough as a royal hoedown, by invitation only, of course, with the lofty queen of angels intended to be the most prestigious prize, soon escalated into a newsworthy block party, a flash mob, and a showdown, while the lordly lords-a-leaping who were lording over modern science and modern medicine swaggered, postured, and paraded all about, and while the sharpest of the sharpshooters, the visionaries, the imaginers, the charlatans, and the impersonators arrived one by one to witness and/or participate in the impending contest.

"By tragic necessity, with both medieval jousting and card playing in the Wild, Wild West, the showdown inevitably became a decisive show-and-tell-all *throw-down*, one that brought with it the undeniable stench of rotten eggs, along with telltale images of certain death looming, thereby diminishing any illusions of safety held by anyone lurking behind dark curtains, peering meekly through venetian blinds, or hiding timidly behind watering troughs, enlivened by an eye-opening, knee-knocking, heart-pounding fear that comes to those who face the sudden swinging of the saloon doors at high noon with nothing but their own bodies shivering, their own saliva drooling, and their own unbearable sadness at having zilch in their hands.

"With lifetimes burning as bright as Southern California sunlight, and with Boot Hill growing fast in clear sight, there simply had to be a decisive, nail-biting, jaw-tightening, gut-wrenching standoff—on Sunset Boulevard, no less. The daring throw-down led to a public *beatdown* of all the poseurs: all the mindless, careless, and militant, and/or malicious-minded individuals assembled from nearby buildings and city blocks, including the latter-day dandies touting modern-day science and/or sci-fi facsimiles thereof, who were confronted with a timely demonstration of logical positivism by way of the biotechnically advanced Clovis point modeled on the one of antiquity. This is this very same Clovis point that you, Everett, now carry for Miss Beatrice."

"The Clovis point is a uniquely American invention!" The voice of Trenton Dostoyevsky, PI, sounded gruff from under his fedora. "It strikes deep! Holds fast! Nothing like it!" he barked.

"Hey, you're supposed to be sleeping," Everett said, scolding him. "Quit interrupting the storyteller!"

Sitting upright, Everett spoke directly to the orator. "I get it so far, Henrietta. In fact, I'm rather enjoying this deep-dish allegory of yours. However, if I followed your dramatic introduction correctly, you promised to thrill me with a showdown that includes a throw-down, a beatdown, and a slap-down. And while your story of the western throw-down leading to the beatdown of the poseurs and dandies is very entertaining, you failed to mention anything about the epic slap-down as promised. And according to my postmodern *Merriam-Webster's Dictionary*, these three terms do not mean the same thing."

"He's right, Henrietta. You left out the best part when you left out the epic slap-down!"

"Hush, you! I'll explain the epic slap-down to Everett in a moment. But first I have to visit the restroom. Perhaps I'll pause my storytelling for a few moments to make everyone who is still sitting upright a cup of tea." Henrietta gracefully rose to her feet and walked toward the rear of the fast-moving railcar with the enticing confidence of an attractive femme fatale who knows who she is.

"Worth waiting for, Everett." The tough-guy PI laughed from under his hat. "The epic slap-down on Hollywood and Sunset Boulevards is my favorite part of the story."

Everett gazed upon the line of dark and empty windows that appeared like mirrors in the faint light. The distinct smell of jasmine filled the parlor car, its aroma redolent of something exotic.

"As I was saying," Henrietta began again, decorously seating herself with a cup of jasmine tea in her hand, "the aforementioned throw-down and the beatdown occurred when the Clovis point was made visible by way of an inspired intellectual collaboration on Sunset Boulevard, of all places, Everett. You see, amid the royal jousting of the financial titans, the biomedical tycoons, and the academically inclined, amid the many would-be financiers and the privileged pretenders in the vicinity of Hollywood and Sunset Boulevards, one would arise at such a special place and sacred space as this—where bluebirds always sing with joy and dreams surely do come true. One would rise and dare to demand in public: '*We, the capable ones, cannot honestly declare something to be biomedically true that we have not yet formally demonstrated!*' Thus, by announcing the demands of a verifiable Truth, vis-à-vis the cunning Artifice of a biomedical pretense, the declaration of a postmodern molecular/genetic God contest was on!

"In the resulting melee, the scramble for biomedical cover was intense, of course, with titan and tycoon teeth grinding, golden parachutes flying, unclean hands being characteristically wrung or compulsively washed, eyes squinting at the sunset, mouths drooling, and bodies quaking in dismay of the many pretenders amid the dreaded fear of a verifiable truth and/or comeuppance!"

"See, Everett," Trenton said, "I told you. The epic slap-down comeuppance is my favorite part!"

"Hush, Trenton, or I won't continue," Henrietta warned. She calmly sipped her jasmine tea.

"Hush, Trenton, I'm enjoying this!" Everett said, echoing Henrietta. "Please continue, Henrietta. I'm waiting patiently for the epic slap-down. And I already finished the jasmine tea you made for me."

"Very well, with brevity: We know that the Clovis point is a real historical thing, an ancient invention, a projectile that enabled early hominids on the North American continent to hunt large game, including woolly mammoths. Now, in terms of our three-act showdown on Sunset Boulevard here in the twenty-first century—that is, the throw-down, the beatdown, and the slap-down I previously mentioned—the Clovis point is a metaphorical instrument of conveyance and delivery at the cutting edge of the field of biomedicine. Much like you, Everett, the Clovis point is simply a symbolic instrument of conveyance."

"What in the world are you talking about?" exclaimed Everett. "Is the projectile in this fancy briefcase real or not, Miss Henrietta Haddonfield from the human resources department?"

"This new-fashioned Clovis point spells clinical efficacy, Everett. It enables clinical efficacy—the first, and so far only, proof of its kind. The molecular engineering of this new-fashioned Clovis point empowers targeted medical delivery, for it embodies the consummate skill set of the most primal hunters of the animal kingdom. As a primal hunter, the biomedical Clovis point seeks out its quarry within the uncharted territories (and tissues) of otherwise incurable human disease. Standing stationary, as in solid-state bandages, it captures endogenous stem cells and prepares them for purposes of advanced wound healing, repair of damaged cardiac tissue, and spinal cord regeneration. Once the biomedical Clovis point was set in motion kinetically, it proved, at long last, to extend a vital principle of pathotropic (literally, disease-seeking) tissue targeting into the mammoth body *or corpus* of modern medicine—a vital principle for all to see, understand, and freely employ in the future of medical praxis.

"And this awesome feat of intellectual derring-do, this enlightening proof of principle, was performed openly, honestly, and with consummate skill—on Sunset Boulevard, of all places, Everett—with a decisive *snap* and a humiliating slap delivered with authority to medical scholars with a patent-leather glove such as the one I hold in my hand."

Henrietta emphasized the point by raising her white gloves in the air and waving them with a supremely confident flourish, one of the white gloves swooshing, the other slapping.

"The aforementioned slap-down," Henrietta said, reading from her ledger, "was met with fierce opposition from the lords-a-leaping, as one might expect. They all came, of course, to see the Clovis point in action! They came from far and wide to see the remarkable targeting projectile perform its neo-biomedical feats of derring-do—for big ideas they had in abundance, but none of these had been clinically proven to be as effective in the real world of flesh, blood, and bone.

"They came from San Francisco, from San Diego, and from the universities of greater Los Angeles. They came from many prestigious eastern colleges and from the Mayo Clinic to critique and/or witness the obvious: the successful transition from the biomedical bench to the patient bedside, which was a *fait accompli*. They came from far and wide to judge, dismiss, and/or deny, while witnessing the undeniable truth of the matter: the Clovis point had been made once again—on Sunset Boulevard, of all places—and that drew big crowds!

"And then, when the crowd of critics and judges was of sufficiently large size—and with each being of royal enough bearing—to bear witness to this astounding proof of life that had stood the test of time, the principal investigator, lead director of research, slowly raised his left arm and flexed it, presenting his elbow to the baffled onlookers, who were more or less expecting to see a medical magic trick. As the tension mounted, the principal investigator slash director of research placed the index finger of his right hand on the tip of his raised elbow and waited, and waited.

"He waited until the crowd drew near to investigate the curious bend of his elbow, which was meant to mimic the shape of a type 1 beta turn in a key regulatory phosphoprotein, nothing more, nothing less. And then, when everyone who was anyone was standing close enough to see the elegant molecular cybernetics of stem cell survival and control that had just been revealed, the research director extended his flexed elbow explosively, in the blink of an eye, and let loose his patent leather gloves, slapping each of their smug faces in turn. It was a situation of *slap, slap, slap* that was every bit as surprising and as poignant as Humphrey Bogart's in *The Maltese Falcon*; it was an epic slap-down, Everett—an epic slap-down that is still heard and felt around the biomedical world.

"If I could add a personal note, a romantic and humanistic moral of my own, to this mythic tale for you, Everett, it would be this: I believe that inspiration and creativity, which comes naturally from a wholehearted, well-led, intellectual collaboration of inspired individuals, always seems to outperform the devious devices and connivances of institutional orthodoxy and/or unchecked privilege with their cultures of collusion, exclusion, and exploitation." Having ended her Wild West tale, Henrietta Haddonfield, HR, closed the cover of her official ledger.

"Thank you, Henrietta. What a wonderful, refreshing retelling of a classic showdown scene in a western movie. How about you, Trent? You're a worldly, metro-western, hard-boiled American PI guy. You got any ancient cowboy wisdom to add?"

"Yeah, don't squat with your spurs on!" he said, then chuckled from under his hat.

"That's a good one. Got anything else?" asked Everett, smiling up at the unlit chandeliers.

"Yeah. When in doubt, let your horse figure it out."

PART II
TENDING THE WOUNDED UNDER FIRE

Chapter 4

Breakfast aboard the fast-moving *Sunbeam* turned out to be both a blur and an unanticipated delight. The *Sunbeam*, it so happened, was the official appellation emblazoned on the side panels, the ashtrays, the coffee cups, the crystal water goblets, the napkin rings, and the doilies of the restored luxury Pullman parlor car in which Everett found himself, currently dining at a solid mahogany table along with Trenton Dostoyevsky, PI, and Henrietta Haddonfield, HR, while constantly rumbling and rocking, rolling fast on the parallel tracks of the Southwest Chief, traveling in a counterpoint direction, back to the Northeast, with all possible speed, having passed the night and the early morning hours traveling through Arizona, New Mexico, and the Rocky Mountains of Colorado following the path of the Santa Fe Trail that had been blazed by the pioneers of the North American frontier, forged by their dreams, their blood, and their wagon trains. Not much to see in passing; more to remember and reflect upon historically.

"Thank you, Henrietta. This breakfast you made for us is just like a real home-cooked meal."

"*Je vous en prie,*" Henrietta replied, speaking politely in French, then nibbling on a slice of toast.

"And you, Trenton. This cowboy coffee with the early morning bitters is truly hard core."

"Glad you like it," said Trenton, his mouth full of scrambled eggs. "It's the combination of natural ingredients all working together. That's mainly why you're feeling bright and spry with the morning bitters. You see, the roasted then boiled coffee beans that perk us up each morning are incomplete without the bitter fruits surrounding the bean, which help you to grow some brains, help you to preserve some memories, and help you to carry your load."

Everett looked to Henrietta, who affirmed the biochemical analysis by nodding in agreement.

"Look, Trenton, while you're educating me about old-school bitters, I'm sitting here casually eating with one hand—linked to this heavy-duty attaché—figuring brightly, or not so brightly, what, if anything, this aristocratic attaché has to do with the Clovis point password and the 'Fram has sailed' dispatch you sent to Miss Beatrice. Could you fill me in on any of that?"

"Frankly put," Henrietta Haddonfield said, "the Clovis point is in your custody, Everett. And because of your forthright dedication to this special private mission that you previously arranged with Miss Beatrice, we can officially confirm that, indeed, the Fram has sailed."

"The Fram being me?!" Everett exclaimed with reluctance.

"The Fram being you," Trenton Dostoyevsky, PI, answered. "You see, Everett, in our line of business, that business being true crime, punishment, and comeuppance, there are only two mistakes one can make on the road to truth: not starting, and not going all the way!"

"Thanks for the freaky metaphors and the scary moral imperatives, Trenton. But I've been to a library or two in my time at the university, and I've heard similar cautionary words before. Sounds to me like a core idea of Tibetan Buddhism."

"It just so happens," the hard-boiled PI character responded, belting back a swig of orange juice, "Mister Tambourine Man, that private investigators like me have a hard-core respect for truth, nature, and reality just as it is, more so than for personalities, opinions, and the conveniently self-serving connivances of evildoers who distort the facts of a given matter for their own advantage. But, alas, as much as I strive to be an accurate representation—nay, the epitome—of a Dash Brogan private eye and a revealing moral force of nature, I continue to fall short of practicing any kind of serious Buddhism, old sport."

"And why is that?" Everett asked, expressing more than a casual interest.

"Ask her. She'll tell you." Trenton pointed a thumb to Henrietta Haddonfield.

"Well, Henrietta?" Everett asked.

"Right speech! He doesn't have it, Everett. He certainly doesn't practice it—among other things." Henrietta smiled discreetly, shaking her head with feigned disapproval.

"OK, folks, I think I get the picture. I'll ask you, Henrietta, to tell me more about the Fram, which is an odd egg-shaped sailing vessel that sailed into history a long time ago, as far as I can remember. And then I'll ask Trenton to fill me in on the real story behind the Fram allusion in his own colorful and humorously hard-core, if not technically and philosophically improper, vernacular."

Henrietta opened her ledger and read carefully. She inhaled deeply and slowly exhaled several times before speaking. "I'll begin by reminding you that the Fram, a polar research vessel, was uniquely suited by intelligent design and enlightened intentions to convey its precious cargo of human accomplishment beyond the boundaries of discretion. Much like you, Everett, the Fram was designed to proceed and not be crushed—designed to endure, to hold together, and to succeed on a special mission of epic proportions. Much like you,

Everett, the *Fram* was tested and proven long before it was revived, reoutfitted, reoriented, and launched on an impossible mission with limited human resources, against the odds, against the prevailing principalities, beyond all previously known bounds."

The decorous swiping of a white linen napkin from her lap, then the patting of it to her luscious lips, signaled the end of Henrietta Haddonfield's introduction to the *Fram* as a vessel and an abstract instrument of conveyance.

"It's your turn, Trenton—your turn to spill the beans, your turn to open up and come clean, *s'il vous plaît*. It's your chance to explain to me bluntly, in any vivid hard-core PI shoptalk you like. It's your chance to explain graphically, with whatever shocking; sarcastic; spiteful; disturbing; hard-hitting; knock-down, drag-out; overly expressive speech you choose to use. I'm asking for the real scoop, the true story behind this *Fram*-has-sailed allegory that you and Henrietta mentioned explicitly in your dispatch to Miss Beatrice."

"Do you even know what you are asking me, Everett?"

"I'm asking for the hidden meaning behind your tactful dispatch. I suspect that it might be a commentary on me and/or this mission that Henrietta dispatched to the lovely Miss Beatrice. Now it's your turn, Trenton, *s'il vous plaît*. It was your allegory, verbally communicated to Henrietta, that was officially dispatched, as I recall."

"Well, since ya put it that way!" Trenton Dostoyevsky started to explain, but not without glancing quickly at Henrietta Haddonfield for her OK, with her subtly nodding back in approval.

"The first point to remember is that the *Fram*, meaning 'forward,' was designed for extreme polar exploration. The three-masted Norwegian schooner was expertly crafted for a bold mission to prove a scientific theory, namely that polar ice floats, yet on this polar mission, the craft failed to float precisely over the North Pole. Not long after this, Commander Robert Peary of the US Navy claimed the coveted prize for the USA amid royalist outrage, medical fraud, obstinate academic finger-pointing, and global incredulity. Yet the intrepid Norwegians—who built the *Fram* and who had gotten frozen in the ice after having floated tantalizingly close to the North Pole—learned in their failure not to trust in theory, luck, or bloody awful politics. Together, they learned not to trust the naysayers who were asserting that Commander Peary and his motley American crew shouldn't have, and thus couldn't have, succeeded, and therefore they must have lied. Together, the polar explorers who built the *Fram* learned not to trust the official narratives."

"What else did the explorers of the *Fram* learn in their failure?" Everett queried. "And how did they finally succeed?"

"Good question, Everett. Means you're paying attention. What and how indeed! You see, it's not what the royal detractors said about the North Pole's not being officially discovered, but what they did consequently! It's what the lordly lords-a-leaping did subsequently that set things in motion concerning the *Fram*'s next polar expedition. You see, Everett, right after Captain Robert Peary called in his official report to say that he had reached the North Pole, the not-so-sporting blokes of the British Empire claimed for themselves the last remaining global prize—the South Pole!

"After that, the Antarctic continent was considered off-limits for exploration, with visits there reserved as a prickly privilege of the British Empire and its royal aristocracy, its exploration protected as a birthright reserved exclusively for overlord imperial chaps, thereby preventing international competition, placing restrictions on new funding for exploration, and denying sociopolitical permission for the intrepid explorers of the egg-shaped *Fram* to sail forth again. And yet they did sail forth, to the South Pole, virtually alone. A grand obsession can be like that, both passionate and possessive."

"Go easy, Trenton. Your tale of tall ships and competing egos is getting personal."

"I can see your point, seeing that you're the man with the herculean task at hand."

"That's a bit Greek to me, Trenton. Can we get back to your story of the *Fram*?"

"OK, old sport, fasten your seat belt! There is another part of this story that you need to hear. It's generally not what people in positions of authority will tell you is permitted or true, it's what you can discern using your own common sense. You see, the intrepid Norwegian explorers realized that the Americans had indeed reached and laid claim to the North Pole. It was only the deflated Englishmen and the pipe-smoking curmudgeons of the Royal Geographic Society who couldn't handle the truth. Therefore, they failed to learn the methods of the American A-team, who were the first to drive dogsleds to the top of the world. *To learn from the success of others—to learn and to progress—or not to learn: that is the biggest challenge!* One can only imagine the passion for exploration revived when the savvy explorers aboard the *Fram* cleared the political docks, reoriented their chart room, informed their crew, and committed their egg-shaped vessel to the Antarctic voyage south. The crew were elated. For in so doing this, they were laying claim to their own ambitions, sweat, toil, and drudgery; blazing a trail with their own original footprints; and working together as a well-led team in the blinding snows of history."

"That's a cool history lesson, Trent. Your sarcasm and your *Profiles in Courage* approach to international relations is totally off base, but I suspect that there's more to the story here!"

"Yeah, Everett? And just how far does your suspecting intuition take you? Give it a shot!"

"I suspect that the true story behind the *Fram* is what the Norwegian explorers figured out with their own discerning minds—that the American team had indeed reached the North Pole!"

"Bingo!" Trenton exclaimed, smiling and nodding his head in approval.

"Well done," exclaimed Henrietta. She opened her ledger to read again. "Alas, in the context of human resources and epic accomplishments, those in power tend to exhibit a fatal flaw when they collectively agree to uphold a self-serving lie. Unfortunately, much like Oedipus, the king with unconscious desires, these people often don't even realize when they are doing it!" Henrietta continued paging through her ledger as though she were looking for something specific. "Aha, here is a prime example: '*We will drive you out! We will spend you out! We will wait you out!*' This is a verifiable threat made against any and all independent academics, driving intellectuals, adventurers, and explorers away and/or deeper underground—like so many unpaid pipers, who leave only a few strains of their beautiful music behind for future generations."

"I like the part about the unpaid pipers, Henrietta. But I'm still waiting for a punch line, folks. And if you like contemporary music, then you know that the waiting is the hardest part."

"The point that Henrietta is alluding to, Mister Delivery Boy, is that they will wait you out! Google it for yourself! Even now! It's been more than a century since the Arctic explorers came and went. In the meantime, the eye-blinded oedipal geopolitical top brass compounded their offenses with armchair analysis and deadwood devious intentions, funding blue-ribbon naysayers and rented snowmobilers with slushy opinions, distorted rationalizations, and incompetence. They're still doing this now, long after the Peary team laid down the expeditionary facts, with records, dates, and photographs to prove that their expedition had been a success."

"Now I get it! At least I think I do!" exclaimed Everett. "The real scoop and the true story is there in the records and the photos! It's still there to be seen, and it will always be there, as official, permanent, and historical as an album cover!"

"Sounds to me that Miss Beatrice chose the right man for the job, Henrietta. This washed-up and sometimes clueless songwriter has a least half a brain to reason with. Now, if you'll pipe down, Everett, we can finish this debriefing and get on with our day. What do you think, Henrietta? Do you want to explain the science of forensic photogrammetry to Everett, or do you want me to extrapolate the far-reaching astronomy more graphically?"

"I'll do it without any of your jaundice or sarcasm, *s'il vous plait*." Turning to Everett, she explained, "Forensic photogrammetry is a modern scientific method for determining the sun's position from photographs. It was recently used to end the debate about whether Peary's team actually made it to the North Pole or else faked it, as some have said that they missed the mark by one hundred kilometers. In opposition to the Global Geographic Society, a distinguished group of professional navigators came forth to perform the analysis and dispel all doubt. Using spherical trigonometry to measure the Artic explorers, their flags, and their shadows, the forensic navigators determined the declination of the sun when each of the photographs was taken. It is a complex calculation, I am told. The technique is called photogrammetric rectification, where one draws a line from the tops of any objects in the photograph through the tops of their respective shadows. By using the same principle that artists use to determine the perspective of a painting, the convergence of lines at a vanishing point below the horizon indicates the angle of the sun's rays in a rather straightforward and scientifically revealing manner."

"You mean just one look at a photograph of the American A-team standing together at the top of the world and the professional navigators could tell that the dismissive royal narrative was false?! They could tell by the angles and the shadows? That's even better!"

"Pegged the Pole within a stone's throw," Trenton barked. "On a moving ice sheet no less."

Turning a page of her ledger, Henrietta said, "According to the president of the Navigation Foundation, Commander Peary was not a fake or a fraud, and he did reach the North Pole. He was where he said he was, when he said he was."

"I never realized that album covers could be so important in terms of our cultural history."

"OK, funny guy. Let's see what you learned from our little history lesson. Considering point one: you are the egg-shaped *Fram* of the day. Point two: that *sac à depeche* attaché actually contains the Clovis point in question. And point three: you are carrying some serious social responsibility for a lyric poet, whether you realize it yet or not!"

"I hear you, Trent. And I appreciate the quasi-historical heads-up. Considering that there is a lot riding on this, along with a whole lot of uncertainly on my end, what do you recommend I do?"

"I recommend this: If you're going to try, go all the way! Otherwise, don't even start!"

Everett couldn't help but laugh out loud at the familiar line from Bukowski's *Factotum*. He was also laughing at himself.

Henrietta Haddonfield chimed in: "It could mean losing girlfriends, wives, relatives—"

"And maybe even my mind," Everett asserted with a delighted peal of sustained laughter.

"It could mean not eating for three or four days," Trenton warned in a deep tough-guy voice.

"Ah, 'twas nothing," replied Everett, brushing off the ordeals of his previous travels off the grid.

"It could mean freezing on a park bench," Henrietta warned.

"At least I'll always know where to find chewing gum," Everett quipped.

"It could mean derision. It could mean mockery. Are you ready for that, dude?"

"I've already been derided, mocked, threatened, and isolated from society, folks. And now, if I'm interpreting the history lesson and these prose passages correctly, I conclude that you are both officially advising me, in the courageous manner of Charles Bukowski, to go all the way!"

"That would be our best advice, champ," said Trenton Dostoevsky, PI. "Now, let's take a break to digest our food and stretch our legs before we retire to that fancy parlor with the scenic view. I have one more point to clue you in on, Everett, this one concerning the wiles of history and your own VIP conveyance. Before that, I'll help Henrietta clear the dishes while you freshen up."

Standing upright and stretching his large frame, Trenton Dostoyevsky, PI, silently scanned the scenery outside the railcar, looking on both sides of the train, before he turned back around. "When you get a chance, Everett, you might want to have a look out on the back porch of this fancy railcar that we appropriated for Miss Beatrice. It was designed for American presidents campaigning off the rear platform. You'll like the perspective, looking back across the broader span of US history. It's quite a spectacular view!"

Everett poured himself into the deep plush upholstery of a velvet armchair, placed the black box leather attaché with its chain on his lap, and looked out over the empty prairie. He was immediately struck by the openness of the terrain, the flatness of the land with its tallgrass, and the miles and miles of gently contoured hills and open space.

A large freestanding billboard depicting a circus tent came briefly into view: something "awesome, majestic, stunning, and marvelous" was coming soon, featuring "clowns, jugglers, wild animals, and circus performers." The billboard passed by in a flash before Everett could make out all the words indicating the coming attractions. The empty vistas, the stunning openness, the flatness of the prairie, and the tranquility of the rolling hills returned.

"Right about now I should be reminding you to set your timepiece ahead by two hours, Everett, but I notice you aren't wearing a watch." Trenton Dostoyevsky, PI, was sitting nearby in a matching velvet chair with his snap-brim fedora resting on his knee.

"It all too quickly becomes a blur for me, Trenton, this underground railroad I'm rolling on, this emptiness surrounding me, and this speeding train that is not that much different from traveling on an alternative rock and roll tour bus—although this particular attaché I'm saddled with today feels a whole lot heavier than a guitar case."

"I'll bet it does. But I want you to know, you're not alone in this, Everett. We're here to help you. An important point of our little history lesson is that Commander Robert Peary of the US Navy did not make it to the top of the world alone; he labored shoulder to shoulder, time and time again, with an intrepid friend and colleague of his choosing named Matthew Henson, an African American seaman who from a young age had been trained and educated by a sea captain, who later befriended Robert Peary, and was tested under extreme Arctic conditions before being selected by Commander Peary as first mate on his team's final expedition to the North Pole—with Henson's having been chosen, according to Commander Peary, for his extreme capabilities in the field of Arctic exploration and his loyalty as a friend."

Everett nodded, indicating that he had gotten the gist of the pep talk: teamwork.

"My final point of US history, to put it bluntly, is this: regardless of the reindeer games and the nationalistic and racial injustices afoot, when a football team rises to the point of winning a coveted Super Bowl title, an admirable historic accomplishment, *everyone* on the winning team receives a Super Bowl ring."

"I totally agree, Trenton! *Go, A-team!*" Everett shouted out. "As someone who stands on the sidelines and only sends in the songs, I couldn't agree with you more. By the way, Coach, I keep seeing these random billboards saying something about an old-fashioned circus, or some such thing, coming somewhere soon."

"There'll be more signs."

"When?"

"When we get closer."

"Closer to what, Trent?"

"Closer to the three-ring circus of Portentous Gernikus, old sport. Now that you've had your official history lesson, you should be ready to assist the Magnificent Stymie, star aerial acrobat, in performing his amazing feats of derring-do in the primal RNA world. It's billed, along with of the origin-of-life biosciences, as *The Greatest Show on Earth*!"

"Why would I want to assist the Magnificent Stymie in performing his amazing feats of derring-do when I haven't even the slightest idea what Stymie's amazing feats might be?" Everett asked casually, resting comfortably in the plush velvet-upholstered parlor chair.

"Because that's precisely where we're heading to deliver the goods, Tambourine Man, the *VIP conveyance* and the allegorical *Fram* being you, more specifically, you in the process of delivering the Clovis point, which is safely locked up inside your hermitically sealed attaché!"

"Thanks for trying to explain, Trenton. But I'm as confused as ever. Do I deliver the entire briefcase, or just the Clovis point, which is allegedly locked inside this fancy thing?"

"You'll keep the Hermès case for now, Everett. If and when the Magnificent Stymie performs his amazing feats of derring-do, and if all goes well, we will be safe to proceed to the big top to display the Clovis point system there in the perilous do-or-die high-performance zone, high above the crowds, working without a net, to reach the Open-Air Electrobiodynamic Levitation Pavilion for a final analysis and a final determination. And then, if all goes well, if the molecular arc welding holds and there are no remaining safety issues, the ringmaster and the Magnificent Stymie will have something special to add to that black box leather attaché for you to carry back to Miss Beatrice and company."

"I'm not sure I got all that, Trent. Will you and Miss Haddonfield be there with me?"

"We'll be with you, Everett. This is not the kind of funhouse you want to get lost in!"

They rumbled on through Kansas, the heartland of the United States, with the colors of the setting sun muted by the stormy skies. They rode on until dusk, and then on to nightfall, when darkness sets the stage for something to happen. They rumbled on as billboards gathered to be seen and circus lights winked on.

After some time, the speeding locomotive finally heaved and slowed, with its whistle bellowing loudly, signaling the train's arrival, before caterwauling its high-pitched finale as the train came to a full stop. Following Henrietta Haddonfield, HR, and Trenton Dostoyevsky, PI, Everett descended the steps to be met by a fog-like drizzle. He noticed that the steam engine of the iron horse was gleaming with rain—like sweat—like a wild stallion huffing and snorting beneath the spectral lights of a carnival town, a carnival town that appeared to be spreading out before him like marshmallow frosting on a child's birthday cake.

Trenton Dostoyevsky, PI, led the way through the milling crowds to a staging area along an alleyway, where he moved behind the scenes, glimpsing the murky interiors of what looked to be large wild animal cages filled with shadows and unknown dangers lurking, yawning with wide-open cage doors. They could only see shadows inside the cages, so who knew what dangerous creatures lurked within. Whatever they were, seeing those open cage doors would give any brave man pause. "Guard your thoughts, Everett. You too, Henrietta," the stealthy PI warned, as they moved slowly and cautiously through the shadows. "From this point on, any thoughts that are not good and benevolent can be like wild beasts."

They came upon an unlit circus tent, which seemed odd and out of place even in a back alleyway. The faded sign with peeling paint indicated it was the location of an outdated freak show: *A Wax Museum of Biomedical Oddities*. Such biomedical freak shows, now seen through the lens of history as a bad idea, were once very popular.

"You'll want to steer clear of that tent, Everett, unless you want to see some real nasty things, like a nest of mice living within a child's brain, or a pig's heart percolating out live viruses by the score—mostly pseudoscientific stuff like that. Let's move on!"

No sooner had they arrived at the dressing room door of the Magnificent Stymie than they were ushered inside by Stymie's dutiful female assistant, who promptly positioned Everett beside a large table and directed him to place the black box leather briefcase on the table at an arm's length from all the edges. After handing a pair of dark sunglasses to each bystander, the assistant smiled at the resulting reflections. A moment later, a large, serious-looking fellow, presumably the Magnificent Stymie, without makeup, without his flamboyant acrobat costume, entered from behind a curtain, then stepped right up and handily flipped open the black box leather attaché.

An eerie amber-colored biological glow appeared from within the opened attaché.

"One Clovis point," said the Magnificent Stymie. He spoke with little, if any, evident emotion.

"Check!" the female assistant said in a likewise professional manner.

"Add one purloined operating system from the primal RNA world," Stymie remarked, squinting into the intense amber glow, concentrating his intellectual effort.

"One purloined OS: check!" the assistant replied.

All at once, a fantastic shower of multicolored flecks and bright sparks of light came streaming out of the wide-open attaché. Apparently, the amber-gleaming Clovis point biotechnology, after being conjoined with the purloined operating system from the primal RNA world, became more scintillating and more dangerous—in terms of setting circus tents on fire—when the two primal biological concepts are combined!

"Packaging one open reading frame for the ringmaster!" Stymie worked like a surgeon within the open attaché amid a shower of bright incendiary sparks. "Possible crossover is permanently foiled!" Stymie reported, referring to some obtuse surgical procedure, which was somehow important here. As he worked inside the case, the showers of sparks diminished to nothing until only the soft amber glow remained to be seen.

"Very good," the assistant said in a professional tone. "Now, please adjust the ratios to balance the particles and set the wave parameters for proper transduction."

"Roger that," the Magnificent Stymie replied, continuing to work, squinting into the light.

Everett, removing the dark glasses he'd been given, stepped forward to get a closer look. He watched intently as the Magnificent Stymie lifted a faintly glowing, glittering object into the air with his white gloved hands.

The object he lifted was a sparkling crystalline orb that looked to Everett like a petite myriad reflector, or miniature disco ball. Stymie had lifted it as if it were a precious gemstone. Everett watched as the soft amber glow of the miniature mirrored ball become pixilated in a reflective brilliance with many tiny lights darting and dancing around the dressing room, appearing like so many fireflies. It was mesmerizing. Suddenly, the mirrored ball with the mesmerizing reflections and the figurative fireflies disappeared behind the curtain, along with Stymie and his female assistant, who took with them the mini mirror ball that had shone so sublimely only a moment ago in the star's dressing room.

"You just witnessed Stymie foiling the triple crossover gambit, Everett," Trenton announced. "The rest of the show is a simply a circus spectacle, a.k.a. a formalized public demonstration! Nothing else for us to do now but watch the Magnificent Stymie and his assistant perform their amazing aerial acrobatics." He switched on a handheld flashlight.

Trenton led Henrietta and Everett out from the darkness of the Magnificent Stymie's dressing room and onto the illuminated Grand Promenade of Portentous Gernikus's three-ring circus, where Trenton switched off the flashlight.

They approached the big top with stealth and caution, moving along with the innominate crowd. Trenton led them to three reserved seats in the front row of the bleachers, surrounded by a sea of obstreperous onlookers, way too many to count.

In a moment of wonder, the Magnificent Stymie appeared overhead in full regalia with his now dazzling assistant, dressed to the nines. The crowd roared as each one appeared. The bleachers resonated with excitement and nervous anticipation. The house lights suddenly went dark. To the amazement of all in attendance, the acrobats began swinging, leaping, and catching each other overhead in near-total darkness, the darkness making it difficult, if not impossible, to spot the ropes, the suspended swings, the handholds, or the stable platforms. All that could be seen from below was a faint trail of luminescence, appearing like the tail of a distant comet or that of a falling meteor, catching the human eye with the mesmerizing mirrored ball, its reflective fireflies in action.

"It amazes me how they can do that!" exclaimed Everett. "Catching and swinging and grabbing at things with the house lights off and not ever missing! That's serious acrobatic talent!"

"Some people can see in the dark better than others! Like dogs and cats!" Henrietta shouted excitedly. She was looking upward and clapping her white-gloved hands in delight.

The Clovis-pointed mini mirror ball shined its mesmerizing lights in the darkness just as it had in the Magnificent Stymie's dressing room. It continued to trace the path of the two acrobats, who were swinging higher and higher overhead, while the eyes of the spellbound audience were staring upward, aware of the danger of catastrophe and possible oblivion should the acrobats not find a firm handhold. Everett couldn't help but notice that the Magnificent Stymie and his dazzling assistant were indeed working quite dangerously high up in the air, surrounded by nothing but darkness, and yet they appeared to be working confidently, above the heads of the people in the crowd, without a safety net.

"Get ready, Everett. The Magnificent Stymie is about to climb into the do-or-die high-performance zone, which is even higher above the ground!"

"What is Stymie trying to do?!" Everett exclaimed, hoping to be heard above the clamor of the crowd.

"Like I told you before, he's already done it!" Trenton yelled. "The reverse triple crossover gambit is terribly dangerous if it's not executed just right. The Magnificent Stymie is the first, and so far the only, performer to actually succeed at doing it. The majesty is in the details, Everett! And once the daring deed is duly done, we can all sit back and relax! At least for a little while!"

A single spotlight shone on the dazzling female assistant as she slid slowly to the ground on a long rope. Upon her safe landing, she twirled and motioned with upraised hands, directing everyone's attention to the Magnificent Stymie, who continued to climb the steps of the big top's support pole to breathtaking heights, illuminated solely by the golden spectral firefly flashes of the mesmerizing gemlike orb, which he carried farther and farther aloft with each step he took up the pole.

A second and then a third spotlight winked on, brightly illuminating the dashing ringmaster as he stepped out into the dirt and sawdust of the big top circus ring with ostentatious knee-high leather boots. Everett noticed he was wearing a scarlet-red tailcoat with gold trim, a ruffled white shirt with a bloodred sash, a gold brocade waistcoat, and a showman's black satin top hat.

Shouting into a megaphone, the ringmaster made an announcement to the crowd, emphasizing the extreme dangers involved. And then, as the P. T. Gernikus Circus Band's trumpets played the opening chords of "Entry of the Gladiators," the ringmaster raised his baton, which was topped by a jeweled knob handle, turned it upside down, and held it high overhead. It reflected the circus spotlights, which were intense, sparkling, sapphire blue.

The ringmaster took the sparkling knob from his baton and handed it over to his dazzling female assistant, who immediately began to levitate—with the aid of a pulley and a long rope pulled by a team of horses. Then the rope pulled her up to the perilously high do-or-die high-performance zone, high above the anxious, excited, unruly crowds, where the Magnificent Stymie was already waiting, incredibly high up in the wings.

Stymie's assistant made a theatrical presentation of the sapphire-blue baton knob. Stymie was standing on a platform high overhead as the P. T. Gernikus Circus Band played "Pomp and Circumstance." As this was happening, a cerulean-blue light began to shine overhead and then to sparkle even brighter, which brought a great roar of approval from the clamorous crowd, many of whom continued to voice their pleasure by doing the wave. In the meantime, the dazzling female assistant was returned safely—slowly, gradually, and theatrically—to earth, where she gave an appreciative bow, made a sprightly pirouette, and waved her hand in a dignified way to the high-strung audience, including the VIPs in the reserved seating section.

"Now is the time for you to make your big appearance in the center ring, Everett—out there, where the ringmaster and the pretty lady in sequins and tights are standing!"

"What? Me? What am I supposed to do, Trent? I'm kind of afraid of heights as it is."

"This is precisely what we came all this way for you to try and do, Everett!" Trenton barked.

"It's your turn now, Everett. You can do this!" Henrietta Haddonfield, HR, said encouragingly.

"Now is the time for you to go all the way!" Trenton shouted. "Go on! Introduce yourself to the ringmaster—the one with the top hat! He'll tell you what to do and where to stand! Hop to it, delivery boy. You get to bag and tag that twinkling glow ball in the center of the circus ring for Miss Beatrice!" Trenton nudged Everett hard with his elbow. "Hurry up now! Go on and climb out there, into the very center of things. And, Everett, a little reminder: don't forget the passwords!"

"I don't think I can do this, folks!" Everett exclaimed, standing up and looking upward into the dizzying heights.

Nevertheless, Everett did just that. Inside the big top, he strode into the center of the circus ring with the chain and the empty attaché, which felt much lighter in his hand. He introduced himself to the ringmaster with a courteous bow, then he whispered a password.

The password must have been correct because the ringmaster motioned with élan to summon a gaggle of clowns, who came forth carrying a tall ladder, much to the jubilation of the already overly excited crowd. The clowns as a team set the ladder in the center of the ring and then motioned excitedly without words, like a barrel of mimes, for Everett Durant to ascend it and receive the mesmerizing mirrored ball with its bright blue jewel directly from the Magnificent Stymie—no worries!

"I don't think I can watch this!" Henrietta Haddonfield exclaimed, peering through the cracks between her fingers. Everett Durant bravely climbed the shaky ladder with the empty attaché under his arm. Overhead, the Magnificent Stymie soared and glided, then started to descend.

No sooner had Everett reached the top rungs of the comically tilted ladder—held unreliably in place by a gaggle of circus clowns—than the mesmerizing mirrored ball began to move again, seemingly all by itself, descending from the perilous heights in the darkness, much to the amazement of all, casting a celestial light in passing, appearing from a distance like a brilliant shooting star inside a gleaming golden matrix of fossilized amber.

The mesmerizing gemlike orb, with the sapphire-blue jewel now imbedded in the amber, descended majestically from the upper supports and frame rafters of the big top, looking as if it were the light of heaven itself coming down to earth. As it descended, the orchestra played.

The Magnificent Stymie descended acrobatically from the big top rafters into the public view. Hanging upside down, he circled the big top in a grand, elaborate helical motion, gracefully descended to the lower realms of the circus ring, and glided down upon a shiny black silk ribbon. At that point, the mesmerizing gemlike orb was presented graciously, once and for all, into the palm of his outstretched hand. The Magnificent Stymie zeroed in on the black box leather attaché, which Everett was holding barely open. Nevertheless, Stymie dexterously deposited the orb into the black box leather attaché, and Everett managed to close it.

The gaggle of circus clowns immediately took control of the situation. Collectively, they grabbed the ladder, lofted it onto their shoulders, and began carrying it, tilted, away in a hilarious manner, while Everett was still aboard and clambering to hold on. The clowns continued manhandling the ladder, trying to get the bagman out of the big top in a hurry, scurrying wildly about and tilting the ladder to extreme angles, with Everett barely hanging on. It was a laughable parade of clowns all the way from the big top, to the illuminated concourse of the Grand Promenade, to the Open-Air Electrobiodynamic Levitation Pavilion, designed for purposes of analyzing and making final determinations, or so it said on the giant arched rainbow-colored sign at the entrance.

The circus clowns deposited Everett hilariously, and impolitely, in front of a bizarre array of spinning wheels, levers, and electromechanical contraptions—apparently needed to weigh and measure the potential energy of whatever was inside the attaché, as the determination to either go ahead or not go ahead was usually made by measuring such things as brilliance, luminosity, power, potential, and resistance. Everett was joined by Henrietta Haddonfield, HR, and Trenton Dostoyevsky, PI, who stood helpless as they watched the wheels and dials spinning wildly like so many dinner plates spinning on poles on a stage.

The circus clowns steadied Everett, one of them having him stretch out his arm to full length, then the analytical instruments were clamped onto the leather attaché, thereby enabling the physicochemical measurements.

The crowd applauded with massive appreciation when the illuminated dial of the giant electrobiodynamic potentiometer reached a point well beyond all the prior readings, which was apparently a very big deal. The crowd roared even louder when the recorded electrobiodynamic potential (which is proportional to the resistance) continued rising on a log scale by order of magnitude: from one million, to ten million, to one hundred million, and beyond that, up to five billion potential biological units—electrobiodynamically pegged as a new world record judging by the earsplitting roar of the hyperexcited crowd.

"I guess we passed muster!" Everett shouted to Trenton Dostoevsky, who was protecting Henrietta Haddonfield from the surging crowd. "What's next for us?!" Everett queried. He looked to the private investigator for answers.

"Good time for us to exit stage right, delivery boy!" Trenton barked. The PI motioned with his snap-brim fedora to a large multicolored hot-air balloon with a wicker passenger basket that was tenuously held in place by a series of ropes approximately twenty feet off the ground. The moving spotlights of the open-air pavilion illuminated the fantastic scene. The frantic gaggle of clowns motioned excitedly in mime-like fashion for Everett Durant and his travel companions to continue along with their clown parade to the docking platform, where the hot-air balloon stood tethered and looming.

With the circus clowns all clowning, Everett scrambled up the unreliable prop ladder, the Hermès attaché and its contents in his hand. He was followed, in turn, by Henrietta Haddonfield, HR, and Trenton Dostoyevsky, PI. Once they were all on board, Trenton opened a gas valve and pulled a control lever on the propane burners overhead, which began flamboyantly heating the standing air mass within the hot-air balloon.

Brightly illuminated by the spotlights of the Open-Air Electrobiodynamic Levitation Pavilion, the animated gaggle of clowns gestured hysterically as they unleashed all the ropes that were holding the balloon down and expressively waved goodbye. The massive hot-air balloon rose slowly, majestically, into the murky rain-streaked sky. The frantic circus clowns and the cheering crowds grew smaller, the circus tents grew smaller, and the entire three-ring circus grew smaller and smaller, while the surrounding darkness and the hot-air balloon grew larger. [*Metanote:* HOTAIR is a commanding human oncogene unearthed from the primal RNA world of woe.]

"Nice going, Everett!" Trenton shouted over the rushing sound of the propane burners.

Everett flashed a grin and nodded his head in amazement, holding on tight to the leather-reinforced rim of the wicker basket.

"Time for us to report back to Miss Beatrice, Henrietta!" Trenton shouted. The hot-air balloon continued rising into the overcast sky, to be carried adrift by the will of the winds. "Time for us to inform the heiress that another highly coveted and hotly contested milestone in human history has just been officially realized!"

"How should I word our official dispatch to Miss Beatrice, Trenton?"

"Assuming we are being tracked, I'd suggest an old-school telegram," Trenton said. "Send her something like this: 'Pleased to inform Stymie delivered the goods. (Stop.) The ringmaster provided a bright new star. (Stop.) The troubadour bagged the prize. (Stop.) Landing circa midnight. (Stop.)'"

Chapter 5

The northeasterly drifting of the hot-air balloon over the cornfields of Kansas ended abruptly when the propane gas ran out, the limited supply having been used up to keep the hot-air balloon aloft for hours amid intermittent heavy rains. The descent was alarmingly rapid, one might even say scary, because of the surrounding darkness and the unseen forces of wind, rain, and hail that lashed at and soaked the exposed passengers in the wicker gondola and beat down upon the inflated nylon balloon envelope with a chilling roar, prohibiting any and all upward lift.

The hot-air balloon came down hard at an angle in a large field of waist-high corn, plowing an unsightly swath in the cornfield before stopping and deflating in a jumble. The passengers scrambled for cover under the deflated canopy, guided by Trenton's flashlight.

Everett and his traveling companions from the Dash Brogan Institute of True Crime were shivering like wet rats under the protective envelope of the deflated balloon, while Trenton Dostoyevsky, PI, scanned the makeshift landing zone with the beam of his flashlight, illuminating the raindrops and hailstones from an increasing thunderous downpour.

He continued scanning the area with his flashlight as though he were on the watch, looking for a way out.

"Your life is your life, Everett. Don't let yourself be clubbed into dank submission," he warned.

"I've heard that line before, Trent. In fact, I used to teach *The Laughing Heart*. But lately it occurs to me that you and Miss Henrietta here—and Miss Beatrice, by association—are the ones holding on to the light."

"It may not be much light," Henrietta chimed in, "but as you can see, it beats the darkness." She spoke sternly, trying not to laugh. Failing, she began, ever so politely, to laugh out loud.

The sound of her unbridled laughter, so out of character, caused both Trenton Dostoyevsky and Everett to join in the hilarity, with Trenton switching the flashlight on and off, until they were all exhausted, sore from the unconstrained laughing.

They waited in the darkness for an hour or so, each silent within their own private thoughts, while the restless current of the dithering wind and a drenching rain swept across the cornfields.

A pair of dim headlights appeared in the far-off distance. The headlights seemed to be turning away from the group's location at times, only to return, shining even brighter and more glaring in their general direction, where the three stranded hot-air balloonists were crouched and huddled under the thin protective canopy of ripstop nylon. Everett watched in amazement as the headlights grew larger and brighter, floating over the waist-high cornfields in the haze of this dark and stormy night, winding their way like two lanterns in the pouring rain, moving along some little-known country roads right up to the clear-cut location of the deflated balloon, where the motion of the headlights came to a stop.

Everett could see that the headlights belonged to an old Apache step-side pickup truck from bygone times. The old Apache pickup stood idling in the center of a muddy road less than thirty yards from the deflated heap of the far-flung balloon from the primal RNA circus world. The stranded passengers scrambled from the nylon canopy out into the pouring rain.

A tall and lanky old man wearing a large cowboy-style hat stepped out from the Apache pickup truck and into the mud. After walking to the edge of the cornfield, he lifted his hands to his mouth to project his voice, then he shouted out into the weather-beaten corn: "Howdy, you windblown wayfarers! You folks sure look like you could use a more reliable ride!" The old man stepped up, opened the passenger's-side door, and held it open gallantly, presumably for Henrietta Haddonfield, HR. "Hello, I'm Wade. You can call me Wade," he offered.

Henrietta presented herself, femininely traversing the muddy road with a bombshell smile. She proudly stepped up into the cab of the Apache pickup and pulled the door closed behind her.

After a solemn shaking of everyone's hands, even in the downpour, the man named Wade announced, "You gentlemen can use this tepee tarpaulin as a rain shield!" He spoke loudly, above the noise of the downpour, then stepped up onto the footstep to reveal the hem of a waxed canvas tent. "Oh, yeah," he added. "My Native American peace pipe is stashed with good cheer and some goodies in the large backpack, the one with the bedroll, to keep you high and dry!"

"Thanks, partner!" Trenton shouted, swinging himself up into the bed of the pickup truck.

In the haze of the headlights, Everett struggled to focus and to discern the old man's facial features, which were obscured in the shadows beneath the cowboy-style hat. Staring through the glare of the headlights and the wind-driven rain, Everett thought for a moment that he saw what looked like a pirate's eye patch covering a damaged or missing eye. He wondered which. The old man turned away and started walking back in the mud to the driver's-side door. Everett shouted out, "Thanks for the unexpected connection, Wade! Would you mind telling me where in this watery world we are planning on heading to next?!"

The old man stopped and stood in the rain to explain: "We're planning to run the gauntlet for the lovely Miss Beatrice one more time!" Then he stepped up into the truck and closed the driver's door with a sharp metallic creak and a decisive slam, followed by a brief revving of the engine in anticipation of their immediate departure.

"What does that even mean?!" Everett wondered out loud. He scrambled up into the bed of the truck and secured a position under the tarpaulin beside Trenton, each facing backward, leaning up against the truck cap for support. The old Apache pickup truck lurched forward and drove on in the mist and the rain into the deeper mysteries of the night.

"Would it help if I told you that Wade is planning to run the gauntlet between the raindrops to restore the applied consciousness of Castalia, hidden among the foothills of the Rocky Mountains, where you, Everett, are scheduled to secure a proximal proclamation for Miss Beatrice, along with a cautionary word of warning written upon parchment, a scroll, that bespeaks of the nitty-gritty substratum of a biological saving grace?"

"Put that way, Trent, no, it doesn't help! Not any more than Wade running some gauntlet! Not any more than Stymie defeating the dreaded triple-cross whatever! Not any more than my being here with you and Henrietta Haddonfield in the cornfields of Kansas, with me carrying this Hermès *sac à depeche* attaché hooked on a chain, traveling in the back of an old pickup truck. Not any more than me—"

"I don't blame you for wondering, Everett."

"Wondering what?"

"Wondering why you are still alive, but not yet feeling well."

"Is that what you reckon I'm wondering?"

"Yup."

"You're probably right."

"You hungry?" Trenton Dostoevsky, PI, asked, turning on the flashlight.

"Now that you mention it, I surely am."

"Good news for us, Everett. It looks like Wade packed us some refreshments—snacks, baked goods—along with his peace pipe. The only thing is this: according to my private investigations and the results of the due diligence we performed before staging this off-road adventure, I learned the old guy was once a first-rate biochemist with some serious connections to the Native American peyote religion," Trenton said, switching off the flashlight. "And I've never seen leavened bread glow in the dark like these here luminescent loaves of the elderly desperado's daily bread."

*   *   *

The morning sunrise beamed into a dazzling yet severely limited sliver of clear bright sky, bounded above by a forbidding layer of looming storm clouds that threatened the high plains of Kansas and eastern Colorado with flooding rain and damaging winds. The sliver of sunlight lit up the exposed cargo bed of the vintage Apache pickup truck, warming the coarse fabric of the tarpaulin in a matter of minutes and waking the passengers who were sleeping in the moving truck bed.

Everett awoke to a panoramic view: the first energetic rays of the morning poetically burnishing the blood-tinged canyons, the statuesque red rock monuments, and the iron-bound sandstone and conglomerate fountain formations adorning the Front Range of the Colorado Rockies. From this bloody brilliant and emotionally moving perspective, Everett watched the radiant crimson star fire illuminating the local geologic displays in timeless grandeur, from the silent sentinels of the Garden of the Gods, to the ruddy Red Rocks Amphitheater, to the elite, upwardly thrusting Flatirons of Boulder, to the wide-open yawning sandstone quarries of Lyons and Fort Collins, from which the stone and the stately facades of universities, banks, hotels, country clubs, and medical centers were tastefully fabricated and often uniformly clad.

The approach to the foothills of the Colorado Rocky Mountains directly from the east, heading due west along the Baseline Road, parallel to latitude 40° north, was, in one word, abrupt: physiologically, with the noticeable elevation in altitude, which severely affected one's rate of breathing; visually, with the spectacular eye-opening, mind-expanding progression of colorful vistas; and mentally, from nearly barren high plain flatlands, to the verdant evergreen foothills, to a remote, largely inaccessible world of rarefied air and pristine alpine splendor.

They drove on into an enchanting evergreen forest, passing a series of massive rocks that appeared to be guarding the gates of time itself in this deeply somber forest realm. They motored on deeper into the foothills on an old logging road, to avoid detection, Everett assumed.

The Apache pickup truck came to a stop at what looked to Everett like a western ghost town, a strange ghostlike dereliction of tumbledown structures appearing phantasmal in the parting mist, long-abandoned buildings and only ruined vestiges of a quondam Castalia in the Rockies. The once flourishing community of vibrant, thriving, inspired intellectuals had been abandoned and was now overgrown with unseemly thornbushes, poisonous sumacs, and encroaching vines reminiscent of Angkor Wat, once a thriving city featuring Hindu and Buddhist temples that was overrun by a series of natural disasters and savage political action, leaving nothing but headless statues and the sandstone facades of tumbledown temples to tell the story of a once-flourishing culture that is all but lost.

"I remember a time when this place was alive with the beauty of bright and aspiring minds," Wade reminisced. He walked around the pickup truck and graciously opened the door for Miss Henrietta Haddonfield, HR, to dismount, motioning with a polite sweep of his cowboy-style hat. "It was alive with the carefree laughter of barefoot girls in summer dresses with flowers in their hair," he added with a beaming smile. Wade's hair was wild and uncombed, but his one visible eye was bright and blazing.

"Thank you, Wade," Henrietta said, stepping out with feminine flare. "Please tell me more about this astonishing place." She flashed her disarming blonde bombshell smile at him. Stepping down from the cab, she waved playfully to Trenton and Everett, who were standing together in the back of the old Apache pickup, each silently surveying the devastation and desolation of the once-vibrant Castalian community that now stood ruined, abandoned, and overgrown before them. In the clear morning light, Everett could see that Wade was indeed wearing a leather eye patch over an empty space where his right eye used to be.

"This community was once reserved for the life of the mind," Wade said with authority. "But this particular community of Castalia was no monastic order." He chuckled to himself. "This Castalian community had been established to uphold the highest ideals of scholarship and free intellectual exchange. It was once a mindful, thoughtful place, dedicated to the discussion of esoteric topics ranging from the music of the spheres to the sublime subtleties of mathematics and biological quantum mechanics. It was a place for intellectual discussions of the arts and sciences in the service of the humanities—with myriad nonverbal humanities included."

"Well, something *nasty* must have happened, Wade," Trenton said. "From my perspective, this Castalian community of yours looks dismal and creepy—one might say postapocalyptic."

"You're right about that, Mr. Dostoyevsky," the elderly desperado replied.

Wade stepped out into the expansive overgrown courtyard and led everyone into the grim remains of Castalia like a tour bus guide leading wide-eyed tourists through the ruins of a mazelike campus of tumbledown stone buildings covered over and physically invaded, if not architecturally harassed, by the relentless creeping tentacles of thick poisonous vines that degraded, deformed, and assimilated whatever beauty there once was. "What was once considered idyllic is now regrettably post-lux," Wade lamented. "It is as though the souls of Castalia and her muses—once a wellspring of human inspiration and creativity—is now jaded, barred, and sealed off, separating society, if not humanity itself, from their primal renewing resources."

They walked farther on through the tangled briars and the tumbleweeds into the ruined remains of Castalia.

"I can still remember the shining time when aspiring poets, minstrels, thinkers, would-be healers, and humanitarians from all over the world would gather here, in the humility of intellectual inquiry, in consideration of the highest of academic ideals. They gathered here with the high priests of the great spiritual traditions and with highborn heirs; gathered here with the most masterful of scientific thinkers and theorists; gathered here with the cultural historians and the clinical psychologists of the avant-garde; gathered here with mystical riders on the storm, like me, who came by written invitation in the hopes of comparing notes in holy waters."

"Holy hot tubs, Batman! I get the picture, even without the barefoot girls in summer dresses," Trenton Dostoevsky barked, surveying the desecrated academic temples with his jaundiced private investigator's reality-discerning hard-core gaze. "Something really bad happened here, Wade. Something all too human, if you ask me!"

Everett Durant nodded in agreement, witnessing the same desecration.

"Burdened with pomposity, pride, and a burning desire for any never-before-experienced wanton awakenings, armed with stilted anthropology and self-aggrandizing ideologies—even in the most sacred of places—these Apollonian brutes of privilege, in their permissiveness and downright deviousness, were destructive in their head-over-heels quest to obtain the benefits, the favors, and the elusive creative powers of those yonder Castalian springs."

Everett listened intently as Wade described the ruined academic culture of Castalia in a thoughtful, surprisingly well-educated manner, much like a wise old professor would—which raised more questions than answers. Everett noticed that Trenton Dostoyevsky, PI, and Henrietta Haddonfield, HR, were uncharacteristically reserved and attentive when Wade spoke these strange words, which encouraged further exploration of such matters at a later time.

"'Who knows only his own generation remains always a child,'" declared Henrietta Haddonfield, reading verbatim from an inscription chiseled above the doorway of a grand sandstone building protected by a formidable colonnade of six soaring sandstone pillars standing in a row. Each majestic pillar had remained upright over time, although they were now charred, overgrown, and forbidding, with creeping vines nearly covering the grand entrance with its cautionary signage.

"For what is the worth of human life unless it is woven into the life of our ancestors and recorded by history?" Wade completed the thought paraphrased from Marcus Cicero's *Orator*. "But now is not the time for philosophical reflections, folks. These plague times make it much too dangerous for us to remain in this abandoned place for very long, in clear sight of our many adversaries. Let's go, Everett. Let's go and put that fancy handbag of yours to good use, the one you've been carrying around hell's half acre for the likes of Miss Beatrice!"

"I'm as ready as I'll ever be, *Professor* Wade," Everett said. "But what about my new friends? Aren't they going to run this gossamer gauntlet with me? With us?"

"Your new friends and traveling companions know their limits well enough," said Wade, nodding politely to Henrietta and to Trenton with a blazing one-eyed squint from beneath his cowboy-style hat. Turning to Everett, he said, "Hired guns and professional escorts, no matter how iconic, no matter how hard core, no matter how classy, are simply not invited!"

The man called Wade led Everett away from his traveling companions with a solemn reminder: "And remember, folks, to be aware! There are lions that guard these gates!"

Wade seemed agile to Everett, scrambling nimbly up the steep sandstone steps, passing solemnly through the forbidding colonnade of sandstone pillars, and cautiously entering a level platform filled with deep shadows and broad empty spaces that were hidden in relative darkness. They stopped in front of a great black door.

Wade struck a wooden match and held it up so Everett could read what had been chiseled into the large granite block above the stone doorframe. The flame of the match burned down to Wade's fingertips before Everett could make out all the words, which were obscured by shadows and the chipped granite. As Everett studied the engraving in the match light, the words became clear: "Enter Here the Timeless Fellowship of the Human Spirit."

Wade pulled the wrought iron handle of the great door with both hands. Slowly, the door began to open with a ghastly, unnerving grinding sound. Wade kept on pulling hard on the handle with both hands until the opening was wide enough for Everett to enter the building with the Hermès attaché. Then Wade released the iron handle and advanced straightaway into the unlighted sanctum as the great black door closed behind them with a deep *boom*, like the kick of a bass drum, which echoed through the dark corridors and empty spaces of the deserted building.

Wade struck another wooden match and held it steady to ignite the wicks of two votive candles he had procured from the depths of his coat pocket like a magician. Held together, the two flames barely made a dent in the oppressive darkness surrounding them. The votive candlelight seemed meager, feeble at best, in this sunless, starless twilight space.

Wade handed a lighted votive candle to Everett in silence. It became clear that they had entered a monumental building, although they couldn't make out dimensions, proportions, or scale.

"Are you ready to rock and roll, Everett? Or do you need a moment for your eyes to adjust?"

"I'm ready to follow your lead, Professor!" Everett declared with anxious confidence. The tragic poet gazed around at the dusky maze of unlit empty spaces to avoid staring impolitely into Wade's singular bright, blazing eye. "This outlandish place feels both similar to and different from places I've been before, somewhere at the crossroads of mythology, poetry, and ancient history. It looks like a huge abandoned library, yet this is no library. It feels like a museum, yet this is no museum. It is confusing, like a geometric maze in an ancient cathedral, yet this is no kind of cathedral I can recognize."

"It's called a *labyrinth*, Everett. As dark, scary, and confusing as it may seem to you now, this labyrinth was once a happening place."

"A labyrinth?" Everett asked. "Do such places even exist?"

"Let's get a move on before courage fades, confusion sets in, and our wax candles burn out," Wade said with encouragement. Then he turned away and stepped forward, bathed in meager candlelight, moving onward into the vast pitch-darkness. "Come on now, and bring your briefcase with you. My labyrinth is right this way."

As clearly as light and dark are inextricably connected—in theory, in conscious perception, and in symbolic mythopoetic approximation—the play of the candlelight on the old sandstone walls summoned up voices, thoughts, mysteries, themes, and ideas from the ancient past.

Walking slowly, leading with the feeble light of a flickering votive candle, Wade again quoted Carl Jung, who had astutely declared, "'Man is a Prometheus who steals lightning from heaven in order to bring light into the pervasive darkness of the great riddle.'"

They moved cautiously into the labyrinth lest the flickering votive candle lights falter. "He knows that there is a meaning in nature, that the world conceals a mystery which is the purpose of his life to discover."

From Everett's perspective, Wade appeared to be pushing the darkness away as he moved deeper into the hollows of the unlit labyrinth. Their hands carried the glowing candles through the gauzy layers of some vague material, parting chimerical curtains as they ventured closer toward the mysterious Castilian springs. Wade paused at a crossroads where the pathway extended into darkness in two directions. He removed his cowboy hat and placed it over his heart in a pensive homage to something.

"Are you all right, Wade? You're not lost, are you, Professor?"

"I'll be fine, Everett. It's just that it's been a long time since I crossed over this painful bridge."

"Bridge? What bridge? This is an empty corridor with cobwebs and dust on polished marble floors. Or am I missing something?"

"I crossed this bridge a long time ago, son," Wade said with a sigh. "You see, Everett, there came a time of crisis in my younger years when I was called upon by the high priests of modern medicine and scientific inquiry to perform a sacred ritual of sorts. At this selfsame sacred space, I discovered, much to my dismay, that I was intellectually unable to distance myself sufficiently to place ones I loved, including companion animals, on the sacrificial mercy seat for any reason."

"Mercy seat, you say? You mean, like sacrificing something, as in morality, for science?"

"Something like that," Wade admitted. "I found I was unsuited for being a member of that polite society. This way!" he said, turning decisively and leading in another direction that was equally obscure.

"I think I know something of the sociological deep shit of which thy speak, Professor. So, what happened after you were literally and/or figuratively cast out of that polite society?"

"The monks of molecular genetics and the theoretical biologists took me in," he said as he led Everett down an alternative pathway that took them to his abandoned laboratory. The sign on the door read as follows:

The Proximal Biochemistries of Animal Cell Survival

DANGER: Radioactive isotopes of phosphorus in use

The door opened for Wade without so much as a key. "Don't worry about the phosphorous, Everett. The blazing radioactive material has long since decayed to sulfur. However, the luminous traces of molecular cybernetics revealed by these insightful explorations and experiments in what I call proximal biology will have lasting medical value."

As he spoke, the old professor moved solemnly about the room, lighting a number of wax candles in wall sconces and candelabras set on floor stands. The chalkboard-clad walls of the labyrinthine laboratory were covered with strange modernist/cubist hieroglyphics, elaborate drawings of recognizable figures in distress—something akin to Pablo Picasso's *Guernica*, with the impassive bull and the screaming horses, yet also bearing an uncanny resemblance to the mystical illustrations and visionary paintings of the Romantic poet William Blake.

"Medical value? How so?" Everett asked casually, as he examined the elaborate intersecting symbols, shapes, and lines of these picturesque molecular-genetic hieroglyphics.

"Valuable in terms of healing unhealed bones and even spinal fractures; valuable in terms of initiating tissue regeneration and repair, as regenerative medicine; valuable in terms of hunting down and eradicating the worst kinds of cancers," Wade explained. He placed his votive candle on a large surgical table and motioned for Everett to do the same with the Hermès *sac à depeche* attaché, which he had faithfully carried, handcuffed with the unbroken chain of custody.

"Is this procedure gonna hurt much, Professor?" Everett attempted to jest as his mouth turned dry and as surging chills of mystery, awe, and wonderment ran the gauntlet of his spine.

Wade raised a handwritten manuscript to the light and gave it a good hard final squint like an editor. Then he raised a complex eight-inch-by-ten-inch graphic figure with oblique lines and hieroglyphs for inspection. This one appeared to match the largest of the Picassoesque and Blake-like paintings covering an entire wall of the candlelit laboratory. "This is my *tractatus logico* on proximal biology in its final form, linking cellular respiration and genomic fidelity to stem cell survival via the esoteric biochemistries of a primal and reliable saving grace."

The old professor / erstwhile desperado of Castalia slowly rolled his completed manuscript, including the enigmatic diagram, into the form of a scroll. He bound the scroll with a delicately tied bloodred ribbon, and then, with a decisive flash of his hands, he conveyed the ribbon-bound scroll to the depths of the Hermès *sac à depeche* attaché, with Everett, wide-eyed, assisting in the completion of the operation and in the subsequent closing of the briefcase.

"May I ask you why it took you so long, Professor? I mean, why just now, in these dark times? Why just now is this theoretical work in the life sciences suddenly deemed to be so terribly important?" Everett adjusted his grip on the now closed attaché. "This intellectual work of yours in service of these Castalian springs goes back a long way in terms of your own lifetime, Professor, as far as I can tell." Everett searched the candlelit contours of the elderly desperado's rugged visage, looking over the whole of the once handsome, now injured, and patch-covered face of the scholarly old professor for an answer.

"The announcement of an important truth to immature minds, even with the best of intentions, can do extraordinary harm, Everett," he explained. "We can learn both from the plight of Prometheus and the benevolent humanism of C. G. Jung. Here I quote Carl verbatim for clarity: 'It is therefore important to husband dangerous material very carefully so that first graders do not get hold of dynamite.'"

"I get it!" Everett declared, drawing the latched briefcase back to his side. "This case has something to do with the day of the locusts that Miss Beatrice was so concerned about!"

Everett searched Wade's ruggedly handsome face again in the flickering candlelight for a hint of affirmation. His eyes met the old professor's single bright and twinkling eye for only a moment, and yet in that moment of nonverbal communication, Everett could feel the old professor's tough-minded, hard-core, scientific-eye view soften, barely perceptibly, with the appearance of a reassuring smile that complemented his one bright and blazing eye. Behind the assuring smile, a wise, kind-minded philosophical outlook beamed forth in a genuinely compassionate gaze—even as he beheld the immense sadness, the cultural insecurity, the terrifying existential anxiety, and the medical melancholy of the contemporary world.

Everett felt the additional weight of responsibility on his shoulders as he followed Wade back through the cave-like labyrinth to its entrance. Storm clouds had gathered while they were inside, and a fresh smattering of rain was pounding the ground when they met up with Henrietta and Trenton.

Once again, Everett found himself traveling in the bed of Wade's Apache pickup truck, gazing introspectively at the Rocky Mountain foothills receding into the cloud banks. He was bundled up tight under the cover of the canvas tarpaulin, protected from the rain, heading to Denver's Union Station in a hurry, intending to catch a westbound passenger train.

The urgent dispatch they received from Miss Beatrice was unambiguous:

Please return by CA Zephyr ASAP. (Stop.)

A young surf dude is in deep trouble. (Stop.)

Chapter 6

They rolled into Denver in darkness, peering up at a reimagined neoclassical/Beaux-Arts/renaissance building, where all eyes were stabbed by the flash of neon lights in bold capital letters identifying Union Station and encouraging passengers to travel by train. The black hands of a brightly illuminated clock perched high overhead on an arched parapet pointed to the roman numerals IX and XII. Everett stretched his cramped frame and rolled his aching neck in anticipation. He smiled as he watched Wade exit the cab and escort Miss Henrietta Haddonfield to the curbside with his old-school chivalry. Everett and Trenton Dostoevsky, after that, vaulted from the truck bed without any assistance. A round of hand shaking ensued, followed by the nodding of two professional snap-brim fedoras. After Wade touched his fingers to his cowboy hat in a return gesture, he was gone, just the glow from his headlights in the distance and his two red taillights moving on to another place and time, traveling back into the mist.

"Stay here and act nonchalant," Trenton Dostoevsky growled in a hushed, flinty, directive. "I'll check the front desk and grill the hotel security to see what arrangements might be made for our comfort while we wait for the westbound Zephyr to arrive."

"Do be careful, Trenton," Henrietta Haddonfield, HR, warned, just as she had warned him before upon their departure/descent from the Angels Flight underground railway out of Los Angeles.

"Being cautious yet courageous in the face of danger is my business, sweetheart," Trenton Dostoevsky, PI, quipped, his hands stuffed deep inside his trench coat pockets.

"Then please be quick about it, Trenton," Henrietta said in a demanding tone. "I'm terribly hungry, and I'll need some personal time."

"What about you, Everett?" Trenton growled. "Are you hungry and in need of some personal time?"

"I'll have a cheeseburger and some fries to go, if you can manage it, Trenton," Everett replied. "Besides that, I feel very tired, like I could fall asleep right here standing up."

"You do look a little peaked, Everett," Henrietta said with alarm. The woman studied the pallid face of the tragic poet in the available light while tenderly brushing back his hair and checking the temperature of his forehead. "Please hurry back, Trenton," she whispered anxiously to the PI, projecting her voice like a ventriloquist. "We certainly don't need to lose our only wayfarer to a sudden illness at this point in the rescue mission, not at this penetrating and informative *mise en abyme* reflecting the deeper meaning of Everett's VIP conveyance and his deliverance.

"In English, Henrietta. I'm a self-reflective private investigator, not a French dictionary."

"This *mise en abyme*, this casting into the abyss," Henrietta Haddonfield, HR, said in a soft unruffled voice, "provides a paradoxical mirror reflecting important intertextual clues hidden by Miss Beatrice in terms of her latest underground railroad gambit, reframing the logical imperatives of the Clovis point redemption plan within the VIP conveyance while reenacting thematic elements of the famed Iditarod run to Nome: a historic cooperative life-or-death rescue mission involving both man and beast. Also known as the Great Race of Mercy, or the serum run of 1925, the Iditarod was once a race against time, infection, and supply chain problems to provide enough antiserum to save village children from a deadly outbreak of diphtheria."

"A penetrating *mise en abyme,* you say!" Everett exclaimed, shaking his head and backing away. "Exactly what kind of deep, dark abyss are we talking about here, folks? Seriously?"

"I hear you, Henrietta," Trenton said, ignoring Everett's dramatic outburst. "And I appreciate your symbolism, as well as your human need to pee. Everett here"—he motioned with his thumb—"is apparently beginning to feel the weight of the things he is carrying." Watching the poet standing precariously, he spoke sympathetically. "I'll tell you what: I'll meet you back here in thirty minutes, after you visit the public restrooms. Meanwhile, just try to relax and act casual. And, Everett, try not to glow."

More than an hour had passed before Trenton returned to the designated meeting point outside Union Station. He was carrying some wrinkled brown paper bags. He did not look happy.

"Grim news, *mis compadres*," Trenton announced, taking a seat on an outdoor bench. "The pandemonium has reached us, and it's not safe to mingle or even to go back inside," he warned, handing both Henrietta and Everett a brown paper bag. "There's no room for us at the inn this evening, Henrietta. The tycoons with their minions and aristocrats are all holed up inside the Crawford Hotel, wrapped up in fear and trepidation."

"Where does that leave us?" asked Henrietta.

"Yeah, where does that leave us?" Everett repeated the question, rummaging in his paper bag.

"It leaves us waiting for the next train heading west. It leaves us homeless in the meantime."

"Thanks for the cheeseburger and fries, Trent," Everett said, speaking with his mouth full.

The next morning, the westbound California Zephyr arrived right on time. Trenton Dostoyevsky, PI, promptly ushered Henrietta and Everett Durant to the last railcar in the lineup.

The trailing railcar was noticeably smaller than the gleaming new-fashioned blue and silver Amtrak Superliners to which the vintage railcar was attached. This oddball car was a classic Vista Dome lounge car sporting a prominent observation turret with wraparound glass windows, enabling sightseeing in every direction with a commanding point of view.

Henrietta and Everett boarded the train and immediately climbed up a flight of stairs to the observation lounge, which was decked out in luxurious plush green velvet chairs and linen-covered side tables. Trenton Dostoyevsky, PI, stayed below to discourage any interlopers.

Trenton remained stationed on the loading platform as though he were a train conductor keeping a steely lookout for any mischief-makers. He remained on the platform until the train started moving.

The California Zephyr departed Union Station and hammered slowly through the morning fog, heading west out of Denver with its air horn blaring. Their departure was accompanied by the visceral sensations of two massive locomotive engines working closely together, vibrating intensely underfoot, resonating with a visceral feeling that gradually faded away or rather merged with the exhilarating sensation of gathering speed on spinning wheels, along with a rising splendor of spine-tingling awareness that came from viewing the increasing gravity of the high-altitude landscapes—an awareness that came on with a feeling of suspense that grew ever larger with every elevated mile of the long, slow, serpentine climb of the Zephyr onto the narrow cliff ledges of the Rocky Mountains.

The three passengers traveling *under glass* in the Vista Dome lounge car surveyed their environs as the train climbed upward over rolling plains, up through forested foothills, up to a high overlook that shocked the senses with awe and filled the heart with fear and foreboding at the approach of these impassible mountains—specifically, the direct path by which the California-bound Zephyr was now traveling underground through the Continental Divide.

"Tunnels! More tunnels!" Everett exclaimed. "Ever since I met you folks, I keep seeing myself hurtling on railway tracks leading me into dark tunnels! Arrrgh! I seem to have developed an aversion to the mere thought of entering any more dark and scary railroad tunnels, folks."

"Can't help you there, delivery boy," Trenton Dostoyevsky said, nestling into a deep-green velvet chair with a white linen doily on its headrest. He felt for the brim of his old weathered Hollywood-style fedora and placed the hat on a side table. "There's thirty-some tunnels between here and Salt Lake City, Everett. And another dozen or so after that, I reckon, when we reach the Sierra Madres. Underground railroads tend to travel underground pretty often, as needed, Everett. It's a matter of basic engineering," he added sarcastically.

"Fine with me. I think I can handle the return trip well enough if I'm sitting down." Everett spoke bravely, but as he did so, it quickly became apparent to his professional escorts that he was dissociating, about to enter a fugue state.

"How are you feeling, Everett? You haven't said much since Wade added his proximal proclamation to the Clovis point bijou you've been carrying around in that executive attaché."

"I'm feeling hungry, dizzy, and tired at the same time, folks. That's all I know," he said. "Other than that, I don't know much." He closed his eyes and began mumbling lyrics: "'Don't know much about history. / Don't know much biology. / Don't know much about a science book.'" Slowly, he drifted off to sleep.

"Ya gotta admire the way he shrugs it off, Henrietta. I've seen hard men literally melt under the pressure of possessing such groundbreaking medicaments. Most fall to pieces under the strain."

"I do admire the peaceful way he sleeps, Trenton," she said tenderly. "Did you notice how quickly and how peacefully he simply nodded off?"

"My investigations confirm that he sleeps with imaginary angels, Henrietta. This curious aspect explains a lot about the motivational psychology of our jingle-jangle tambourine man."

"Whether it's imaginary or not, he seems to have found a place of refuge amid his emotional tempests. Look at him, Trenton. There is an angelic quality about the way he sleeps." She spoke softly to avoid waking the sleeping poet. "Can you see it, dear?" she whispered inquisitively. "It's almost as if you and I aren't the only ones comforting and protecting this tragic singer-songwriter, this VIP instrument of conveyance."

"I only have eyes of flesh, Henrietta. I'm trained to view such luminous beings from a safe, dispassionate distance, looking upon every man, woman, and child with the same judgmental disposition to discern their faults, the same uncharitable inclination to view everything in the severest possible manner. When it comes to the luminous world, as you know, I am accustomed to examining outward appearances and visible objects with a bitterness and vexation befitting a man of my profession, my having become hardened by witnessing the extreme violence of the postmodern underworld as it rages on in these dark cities. It matters not to me personally whether Everett sleeps with, or wrestles with, imaginary angels, Henrietta. But it does matter to Miss Beatrice and to the Dash Brogan Institute of True Crime that our designated VIP instrument stays alive long enough to deliver the goods."

Henrietta Haddonfield removed her rain slicker, folded it, and placed it on an adjacent chair. She removed her wide snap-brim fedora and nervously adjusted the ribbon trim. "Do you think that Everett can bear up under the weight of the things he carries on this return trip?"

"He has so far," Trenton asserted. "But I am a little worried about these latest machinations with respect to the mysterious parchment that Wade placed into that Hermès attaché. Everett didn't say much to me about it since we left the tumbledown ruins of Castalia. He only mentioned that Wade was an exceedingly rare kind of professor—a professor of salt and light, he said. Now, exactly what kind of college professor might that be, Henrietta?"

Consulting her ledger, Henrietta thumbed through the pages until she came to one she had previously marked. She began reading quietly for several minutes, interrupted by the occasional dark tunnel.

"Some say Wade was a roadman, whatever that entails in terms of sacred sacraments and Native American spirituality," she said, looking up at Trenton, who was now listening intently. "Some say Wade was a mystic and a biophysicist who could hitch a ride on a beam of light and follow it conceptually, logically, and positively to the beating heart of a single animal cell." She read on from the ledger: "Most experts affirm that Wade was a consummate biochemist—a gene hunter in the gold rush days and a true pathfinder in the primal molecular-genetic Wild West."

After reading silently for several minutes, Henrietta continued: "I can confirm that Wade taught high-level courses on the origins of consciousness and cancers in the most primitive of animals, that is, until some kind of academic dustup. The official consensus is that Wade was an inspired physiologist who brought together a myriad of activating factors, catalytic characters, and powerful unseen forces operating at a distance."

"Unseen forces operating at a distance, you say," Trenton remarked. "You mean like gravity pulling on the planets? You mean like the trajectory of a speeding bullet before it smashes through flesh and bone? That much physics and physiology I can easily understand."

"No, Trenton. It appears that Wade did not merely fight against flesh and blood and bone, but against the rulers, the authorities, and the evil forces lording over this present darkness."

"Come now, Henrietta. You know me better than that. I need details. I need the grisly details. I need investigative granularity, my dear. I need the dirt, the nuance, the true grit. Now spill it!"

"Shush, Trenton, or I won't continue. There is true grit here," she said, "if you behave."

"You win," he said, relenting. "I'll be perfectly silent. I'm a shrunken head with laced-up lips."

Henrietta adjusted her position in the plush velvet chair and continued her summation: "Apparently, Wade and his Castalian colleagues worked for more than ten years in philosophical research and scientific contemplation on this *tractatus logico-philosophicus* on proximal biology, bringing the electronic theories of Albert Szent-Györgyi and the inductive hypotheses of Gilbert Ling to bear on the rate-limiting protein-protein interactions of biological signal transduction. It says here that Wade reached inward, from the membrane of the living cell to the level of DNA activation and immediate early gene expression. It says that Wade succeeded in linking ionic pulses and cascading waves of inspiration to the molecular biochemistries of cellular respiration, genomic fidelity, and stem cell survival."

"Holy smokes, Henrietta. If this means what I think it means, there is no wonder—and for this there is good reason—why the cowboy philosopher scientist roadman character was driven underground."

Henrietta continued to consult her official ledger. "Apparently, Wade and his research team had succeeded in hunting down and characterizing the human growth control genes and the critical biochemistries of a primal, reliable saving grace function. Indeed, they had conceived of, predicted, and hypothesized, ultimately uncovering a proximal rate-limiting point for decisive therapeutic intervention with clinical applications extending from improved wound healing, to tissue and organ regeneration, to more-effective control of aggressive metastatic cancers."

"What happened then? We all know that the rubber meets the road in a car race and that visionary theories of medical cause and effect are ultimately proven out in clinical trials!"

"Nothing happened, Trenton. It says here that the clinical trials were carried out in an orderly and progressive manner. Positive results were achieved at every stage, and the clinical outcomes were all formally published. And yet nothing positive happened. Not for another ten years."

"You mean they hung Wade and his colleagues out to dry? Can you or your ledger give me a clue as to why?"

"No, not exactly, Trent. But it says here that Wade objected stridently in formal publications to the expediency of using of live infectious viruses as a pseudomodern medicine, to be deployed en masse in any therapeutic setting. As a principled principal investigator, Wade insisted that his lifesaving gene-targeted therapies could—and most definitely should—be delivered safely and efficiently by synthetic, certifiably nonreplicative nanoparticles delivered precisely on target.

"It says here that Wade quoted the medical treatises of Hippocrates pertaining to emerging concepts on epidemics [Greek, *epi* (on) + *demos* (the people) = on-the-people]." Then she read the quotation, as follows:

Declare the past, diagnose the present, foretell the future; practice these acts. As to diseases, make a habit of two things—to help, or at least to do no harm.

—Hippocrates, *Epidemics*, Book 1, Section XI, ca. 400 BC

"Wade insisted on safety first in deploying his genetic interventions: 'First, do no harm to the patient, to those who come in contact with the patient, to the human genome, or to humanity itself.' He wrote boldly in indelible ink at the hard-right edge of science and medicine."

"You're telling me that Wade, the visionary roadman and stem cell shepherd who discovered, characterized, and packaged the proverbial saving grace gene ultimately became the sheriff of Medtown?! Ha, that's quite a story, Henrietta. When it comes to Native American roadmen and mystical visionaries lighting up lampposts that no one else can see or even imagine, I'm relieved to hear that a healthy sense of medical ethics comes along with this Wild West territory."

"There's a more recent citation here," Henrietta said while turning pages. "It says that ten years after the clinical trials, previously end-stage cancer patients were still standing upright. Suddenly Wade's avant-garde molecular genetic discoveries became medically compelling."

"I see," Trenton Dostoevsky, PI, said. "And so, if my keen sense of deduction serves me, this survival function is the very thing that spurred the lovely Miss Beatrice to repeat the Iditarod run to Nome, as yet another American relay race of mercy. And that's why we are making a mad dash to the annual big-stick Rattlesnake Roundup scheduled this year in San Francisco."

"Don't be offensive, Trenton! As descriptive as the term 'Rattlesnake Roundup' might be, it is an unnecessarily vulgar way to describe the annual meeting of health-care providers that we are presently making the mad dash to … I would prefer, instead, that you use the term 'Rattlesnake Rodeo,' which leaves some wiggle room for clinical performance."

Trenton Dostoevsky, PI, stood up and looked around to survey their progress, while Henrietta Haddonfield, HR, worked silently, updating her ledger. The California Zephyr swept its way across the American West, reaching the outskirts of the Salt Lake City station by midnight.

Trenton took his place on the loading platform once again, preventing curious onlookers from boarding the vintage Vista Dome railcar, while Everett remained fast asleep at the station. And he remained asleep until Trenton roused him some time later with a selection of prepackaged ready-to-eat meals, prepared in the lower-level galley.

"Rise and shine, Everett! It's time for you to take in some food and water!" Trenton spoke loudly, standing awkwardly while balancing a large serving tray, which he placed on a side table. "I've got a continental breakfast with hot coffee, juice, oatmeal, muffins, cold cereal, assorted breakfast bars, yogurt, and a hot breakfast sandwich. Alternatively, there is a vast selection of gourmet entrées for lunch or dinner, including vegan enchiladas, chicken marsala, and an Asian noodle bowl. Henrietta went for the chicken marsala, but I highly recommend the cheese enchilada with a side salad, if you're thinking past breakfast."

"Thank you kindly," Everett said after sipping the hot coffee from his paper cup. "Where are we?" he wondered out loud. "Did I miss an entire day, or more?" He scanned the wide panorama outside the window. There was nothing to be seen but bleak desert scrubland beneath low-hanging clouds and the vague silhouettes of flat-topped mountains on the distant horizon.

"We're somewhere outside Winnemucca, if that means anything to you."

"It means we're somewhere in Nevada," Everett asserted, looking out the window.

"How are you feeling, Everett dear?" Henrietta chimed in, expressing both curiosity and concern.

"I'm feeling somewhat better, just a little unsettled. Do you think that this fully loaded Hermès attaché will arrive in time, Henrietta, to make a difference for the young surf dude whom Miss Beatrice mentioned in her urgent dispatch? I happen to know a number of young surfer dudes personally, folks. In fact, I have several good friends who follow the waves from Bonaventure Pointe to Half Moon Bay. It's a pretty tight-knit community of avid big wave riders."

"I can't tell you what I don't know, Everett. But at least the young surfer in question will have a choice in the matter and, with his or her informed consent, a newfound right to try."

They were advancing rapidly toward the end of this latest American relay race of mercy, that is, their downhill run from Sacramento to Emeryville, on the shores of the San Francisco Bay.

Miss Henrietta, after making a final notation in her ledger, smiled. She looked up and nodded her head to Trenton Dostoevsky, PI, who immediately stood up, shrugged his broad shoulders, and walked purposefully over to Everett Durant, who still appeared to be in a fugue state, lost in meditative thought or a daydream.

Everett was sitting quietly, looking out the window, bearing up under the weight of it all, when the brutish private investigator adroitly unchained him, the debilitated poet, from the Hermès attaché.

"Well done, delivery boy! You made it to the end of the line!" the private investigator announced with a broad grin—bordering on a smirk—on his face. "Tell him what he's won, Henrietta!"

"Unfortunately, we must leave you now, Everett, in order to complete the rescue mission," Henrietta explained. "There will be a large black limousine waiting for Trenton and me at the Emeryville Station. However, in appreciation of your selfless contributions, Miss Beatrice has scheduled a private ride for you back to Big Sur, along with a VIP reservation at the Wild Thyme Cultural Rehabilitation Lyceum, which includes a personalized health and beauty spa-like experience." As she spoke, Henrietta politely handed Everett a full-color brochure. "Look for the Wild Thyme logo on the side of the lyceum house car. And, Everett dear, fare thee well."

"Are you folks serious?" Everett queried. "I thought that Big Sur was currently an island. How long have I been asleep really? It feels to me like ages, but you say it's only been a day?"

"Sounds like the work of Miss Beatrice to me. Besides, you do look like you could use a health and beauty makeover, old sport," Trenton Dostoevsky, PI, quipped, still grinning confidently, balancing the expropriated Hermès *sac à depeche* attaché squarely on his lap.

The blaring of the air horns announced their arrival at the Emeryville station, accompanied by a long, screeching application of metallic brakes, which brought the California Zephyr to a full stop. In the confusion that immediately followed, Everett watched Henrietta and Trenton disappear into a black limousine. As he wheeled around, he caught sight of the logo on the side of a luxury SUV. He motioned with both hands to get the driver's attention; then, once the SUV had stopped, he climbed silently into the back seat and exhaled. He noticed that the driver of the lyceum house car was wearing a surgical face mask that covered his nose and mouth. Everett decided not to comment. Instead, he leaned back and gazed out at the dim and wavering world beyond the tinted windows.

The question "What's happening?" had been left unanswered. Concerning this, the fundamental point, everything had fallen into darkness, confusion, vague theorizing, and vain speculation. The contemporary scene of desolation surrounding him: was it a fungus, an insect, a gripping miasma, an electrical disturbance, a deficiency of ozone, the morbid offscourings of our culture's intestinal canal? Alas, with regard to sociopolitical undertakings, we knew nothing; we were again at sea in a whirlpool of conjecture.

The return to Big Sur at twilight was a somber road trip, passing the still-life visions of what remained of El Camino Real, the royal roadway established by Spanish colonists to connect all the Californian missions from San Francisco to San Diego. From Everett's perspective, what bleak remains of the latter-day American dreams of freedom, equality, and prosperity could be seen strewn along the fence lines, spread out along the sidewalks, scattered among the urban parks and borderlands, and clustered beneath the freeways. The scores of primitive tents and makeshift shelters floating past the tragic poet's tinted window in the California twilight appeared like clusters of mushrooms springing up after a torrential rain.

Everett reflected on the prescience of Henry Miller, the old romantic reprobate, upon his return to the USA:

You get it at one crack, just walking down the street. The newspapers may lie, the magazines may gloss it over, the politicians may falsify, but the streets howl with truth. I walk the streets and I see men and women talking, but there is no talk. I see wine and beer advertised everywhere, but there is no wine or beer anywhere. On every table I see the same glass of ice water, in every window the same glittering baubles, in every face the same empty story. The sameness of everything is appalling. It's like the proliferation of a … germ.

The term *miasma*, an abandoned medical theory involving particles and foul odors, came to Everett's lyrical mind in his attempt to comprehend or even describe the unpleasant and oppressive atmosphere that emanated from the black workshops, wherever they might be.

It was past nightfall when the house car turned off the main highway and headed into the mountains of Monterey, which served a back door into the wilderness of Big Sur, where any people living there lived off the grid with no electric streetlamps to be seen for miles of rough travel over graded roads that climbed steeply up and wound over mountains before dropping down into deep valleys. The SUV turned onto a gravel road, where it slowed and came to a stop at a clearing in view of a rustic timber-framed shed-roof shelter with a missing fourth wall, where the "interior" space was protected from the elements by an overhanging roof. The masked driver reached back and silently handed Everett a flashlight with a gloved hand. The driver pointed a finger to the open-air shelter without speaking. Apparently, there was no official check-in desk at the Wild Thyme Cultural Rehabilitation Lyceum.

Everett approached the rustic shelter by the light of the flashlight as the house car disappeared into the darkness. There was a single wooden bed, a bedroll, and a solar lamp with multiple power settings. Everett sat and scanned the brochure by the light of the lamp. He read an epigram—"Do not neglect to show hospitality to strangers, for thereby some have entertained angels unawares (Hebrews 13:2)"—and he wondered. Then he turned off both lights.

Alone again, Everett thought as he looked out at the vast surrounding wilderness. His world slowed down until it stopped. Feeling around, he found that all his pockets were empty—no wallet, no phone, no keys, no hidden money, and no scraps of paper with lyrics or passwords written on them. Everything had been provided for him, just like the gossamer heiress had told him. Moreover, he gradually realized, he was no longer chained to the enigmatic Hermès attaché. *What a relief!* he thought.

Everett realized that he was no longer being transported on a speeding locomotive, driven through the narrow archways and reverberating subterranean tunnels of an underground railroad. He was no longer climbing up dubious circus ladders, no longer floating weightless over unseen cornfields in the inky darkness—make that crashing into actual cornfields in the pouring rain! He was no longer traveling in the back of an old Apache pickup truck, no longer a rider on the legendary California Zephyr hammering through the more than thirty dark, scary tunnels of the Continental Divide, and no longer motoring into Emeryville in a great big hurry. He was traveling the lonesome road of one again, sitting all alone with no particular destination in mind, just the reassuring notion that he would meet up again with Miss Beatrice and Manifesta et al. at the Henry Miller Library one Sunday night in the near future. He realized that looking forward to meeting up with someone again with something special in mind—when the limo drives away—was a much better feeling than the lingering emptiness of abandonment that he knew so well.

It was then that Everett realized he was being watched. And not by human eyes. He clicked on the flashlight. Two bright eyes flashed! Everett immediately turned the flashlight off again.

Those were the golden eyes of a small nocturnal feline, a solitary hunter whose tapetum lucidum, located behind the retinas, both captured and reflected ambient light accurately, with constructive interference, thus increasing the amount of light passing through the retinas, enhancing night vision and enabling the nocturnal creature to see such light that is imperceptible to human eyes.

"Welcome, little one," Everett said as the feline creature approached. "Little kitten, if you were any larger, you would have seriously frightened whatever piss and dickens remains right outta me."

The morning sun shone faintly through a veil of maritime fog, its radiant fingers a flimsy moist chiffon covering the dense chaparral, the grassy meadows, and the coastal woodlands of live oak that were dripping with dew and draped with mistletoe.

Everett awakened and opened his eyes at the sound of footsteps approaching on the gravel path. He rose up to a seated position and peered intently into the fog, noticing that the little feline that had visited him in the night had taken up a position at the foot of the bed and was wide awake, listening.

The figure of a mysterious woman with shining black hair came into view. The closer she came to the shelter where Everett was seated, the more stunningly beautiful she appeared to him. He figured it must have been the lighting or the mysterious atmosphere of this strange place. He closed his eyes, rubbed away the cobwebs of sleep, and reopened his eyes to the world.

"There you are, Mister Brody!" the mysterious woman exclaimed, pointing to the little yellow tabby cat with the variegated markings of a tiger. "You had me worried." She said this in a scolding tone as she approached the open-air shelter. "And look, I see you brought Everett Durant a gift offering." She feigned disappointment. "Are you trying to make me jealous, Brody?"

Everett saw that the gift offering was a dead mouse, laid on the brick pavers just outside the shelter. Before Everett could think of a single thing to say, the mysterious woman, who was beautiful, introduced herself. "Good morning, Everett. I'm known around here as Raven. I've come to take you to breakfast and to the showers—reverse that order—and then to show you around this magical place."

"Hi, Raven. I'm pleased to meet you. But I didn't mean to steal your kitten," Everett said, smiling, discreetly admiring her contours and her bearing. "He is good company, though." He pulled on his boots one after the other. "I think I slept pretty well with Mister Brody standing guard."

"Oh, Mister Brody is such a Casanova, always making new friends. Still, I worry about him terribly when he is out all night with the wild things. I'm just happy that he's safe, is all."

Everett studied the face of the woman and noted her pleasing demeanor as she spoke, realizing that she was a natural beauty without makeup—and likely a charmer of men and a potential heartbreaker without even trying.

"Don't be too hard on the little fellow, Raven," he said. "He's only just a kitten after all."

"Mister Brody is much older than he looks, Everett. He was already eighteen years old when he was first brought to this healing place. The poor boy was nearly blind from high blood pressure in his old age, and he was suffering from severe osteoarthritis. It took the best of modern veterinary medicine and the healing arts to restore him to health. According to our records, Mister Brody is more than twenty years old now, which makes him geriatric in cat years."

"Funny, what you just said reminds me of a folk song I remember from long ago. It is a bittersweet song about lost youth, growing up, and growing old."

"You must mean 'Sugar Mountain,' by Neil Young," Raven said, laughing confidently. "A lot of folks around here feel the same way about this place, Everett. Your folk song goes like this: 'You can't be twenty on Sugar Mountain, though you're thinking that you're leaving there too soon.'" She sang the lyrics melodiously in a cappella style. "There, am I right?"

"You're leaving there too soon," Everett concurred.

They walked together along the forest path, with Mister Brody traveling discreetly off the trail.

"Who actually owns this magical deep-in-the-woods healing place?" Everett inquired, while gazing at the sunbeams that were streaming into the misty depths of the live oak forest.

"In reality, no one owns anything but their own dignity, Everett," Raven said self-assuredly, strolling along the woodland path. "However, to answer your question more directly, this US cultural rehabilitation lyceum continues the honorable tradition of adult education. It's named after the meeting place where Aristotle once lectured on topics ranging from physics to biology, from logic to linguistics, from aesthetics to high drama and protopsychology."

The sounds of an ephemeral mountain stream, swollen with rainwater, could be heard in the distance, burbling and rippling as the water plunged over unseen cliffs into clear freshwater pools below.

"The American lyceum movement," Raven said eagerly, "was supported by such luminaries as Abraham Lincoln, who denounced mob violence and promoted adherence to the rule of law long before he ran for president; and Frederick Douglass, a lyceum celebrity who promoted a reformist agenda; and authors Henry David Thoreau and Ralph Waldo Emerson, who would often read their essays out loud at the lyceum meetings *avant la lettre*, that is, before those writings appeared in print."

"Whoa! Whoa! Whoa there, Miss Raven!" Everett exclaimed, waving his hands, stopping in his tracks, and turning to face the beautiful young woman. "I've been hearing quite a lot about Ralph Waldo Emerson and his transcendent ilk lately, ever since I chose to venture forth on this Big Sur wilderness trek. Also, I am fully aware that this Wild Thyme Cultural Rehabilitation Lyceum has something, if not everything, to do with the likes of Miss Beatrice and her benevolent stewardship of one historically vague yet figuratively rich cultural inheritance."

"Oh my. I'm so sorry. Is it that obvious? I was just trying to appear knowledgeable, Everett, considering that you were once a professor of beatific literature and a contributing poet to this generation's avant-garde. I think I have a problem with learning about new things: great ideas, great deeds, great art. I'm always in such a hurry to share any great ideas from the healing arts with others for the sake of truth and understanding. Of course, *you* would know all about the lyceum movement and its democratic ideals from the words of the poets themselves."

"I am familiar with the American lyceum movement that promoted both community education and self-acquired knowledge in philosophy and the natural sciences. It was popular in the mid-nineteenth century. Beyond that, Raven, I'm more interested to hear what Emerson's prose means to *you* and, more to the point, what this latest interpretation of the old-time lyceum movement means for *me*."

Raven giggled shyly and appeared to blush as she explained: "I imagine that news of a speaker as popular as Ralph Waldo Emerson appearing at the Concord Lyceum must have spread like wildfire in his time—much like our contemporary social media. I can imagine Ralph Waldo Emerson reading his transcendent poetry and his inspiring essays in person. First, he lectured publicly in Concord, then he lectured in all of New England. Then the boundaries of his lecture circuit increased, spreading south to Washington, DC, and then across the Midwest."

"That's an interesting perspective, Raven. Speaking as one who has been offline for some time."

"Concerning *you*, I reviewed your medical charts. Your right shoulder was dislocated; you have had a number of fractured ribs, which may or may not have healed properly; and you still have a noticeable limp. I understand that Miss Beatrice has you scheduled for rehabilitation in the form of a ceremonial hands-on healing demonstration later this week."

"A ceremonial hands-on healing demonstration, you say? Seriously, Raven? I've already been through the wash cycle and the rinse cycle, so to speak. Are you sure that Miss Beatrice went to all this trouble to find this place and get me here in a hurry just to offer me a massage?!"

"Miss Beatrice is such a peach, Everett. She provides such generous funds for this magical place, including my apprenticeship in the composition and applications of ancient healing elixirs. In addition to that, I understand that the heiress recently contributed a substantial sum to a local conservancy group so they could purchase a large tract of the Big Sur wilderness and return it to the Esselen tribe of Monterey, who were displaced from their ancestral homeland two centuries ago. And I have heard that you, Everett Durant, are the main reason that Miss Beatrice has acquired this recent compelling interest in American wildlife conservation and cultural rehabilitation."

They began strolling again, both feeling challenged and inspired by the romantic ideals of Ralph Waldo Emerson and his fellow transcendentalists, who believed that a self-reliant, freethinking, nonconforming, and/or intuitive individual might be well capable of exhibiting true originality and creativity worth sharing with others in terms of cultural innovation and continuing education.

The forest path led them downhill, across a dry grassy field, and back into the canopy of the coastal live oak and redwood forest. Mister Brody came and joined them on the forest path. The sounds of the falling water became even louder. They followed the path together as it dropped down alongside a jagged cliff face, where they came upon a dazzling intermittent waterfall with a deep plunge pool, appearing as idyllic as the images one might find in a neoclassical Maxfield Parrish landscape painting, where rain-fed white water is seen gushing out from a mossy overhang of rocks and cascading down a steep channel of water-polished stones before plunging into a turquoise reflecting pool that now beckoned the forest wanderers with the tantalizing possibility of full immersion—with the exception of Mister Brody, who took up a superior position by the plunge pool atop a sun-kissed boulder.

"Is this the morning shower you had in mind for me?!" Everett had to shout to be heard over the roaring sound of the cascading waterfall. "It looks a bit much. It looks a bit daunting to me!"

"No, silly!" Raven laughed, shaking her head as she spoke. "You can take a cold plunge here if really you want to, Everett! Many people do! However, there are modern spa facilities with hot showers, steam rooms, whirlpools, and saunas, followed by a cleansing smoothie and a gourmet meal at the commissary. Just follow Mister Brody and me." Raven giggled as she skipped past the waterfall and its dramatic plunge pool and headed ever so lightly down the forest trail.

Everett watched her feminine movements with amusement, and he smiled as Mister Brody bounded purposefully off the jagged boulders surrounding the plunge pool with the athletic nonchalance of feline parkour: decisive, obvious, and efficient in his headlong free-running quadrupedal effort to catch up with his beloved Raven before she disappeared from his view.

The luxurious sensation of perfectly heated water falling in abundance over his head, neck, and shoulders, while surrounding his naked body, would feel both sublime and reinvigorating to Everett, as it would for anyone, after being strung out on the road for any length of time. He moved with the solemnity of a medieval monk through the lyceum day spa, sporting a hooded Wild Thyme silver-sage terry robe, which he slid on and off again as he moved from the steam room to the hot tub, to the infrared sauna, to the bracing cold lap pool, to the heated showers yet again, in the practiced manner of a monk performing a solemn sacred ritual.

"I ordered you a Green Garden smoothie with an Anti-Everything-Bad chaser," Raven exclaimed with delight. She smiled with approval as she approached the pampered poet in the monk's robe and handed him a tall paper cup with a straw sticking up through the lid.

Everett took a hard pull on the straw, so hard that he risked the dreaded brain freeze that so often accompanied rapid smoothie consumption. "Wow, that is too salubrious for words," he declared with a wide-eyed grimace. "What's with this Anti-Everything-Bad shot you put in here?"

"'Everything Bad' refers to the broad-spectrum bioactive phytopharmaceutical extracts, which fight against natural pathogens such as bacteria, parasites, invasive fungi, and even viruses."

"This Green Garden smoothie sure packs a punch!" Everett affirmed, sipping the last of the smoothie with the slurping sounds that usually accompany the act. "What's in this really, Raven?!"

"Let's see," she said, reading a small ingredients card that apparently had come with the fortified smoothie. "It says here the Anti-Everything-Bad chaser includes a dose of pentacyclic triterpene saponins and flavonoids from the licorice plant, or *Glycyrrhiza glabra*; a dose of the cleansing artemisinin endoperoxide from *Artemesia annua*; a dose of indole-3-carbinol, a bioactive phytochemical found in cruciferous vegetables; and a dose of *Bacopa monnieri*, with its potent terpenoid glycosides. Taken together with the high-potency polyphenols and micronutrients in the Green Garden smoothie blend, the Anti-Everything-Bad chaser is intended as a prophylaxis, a form of therapy, and a restorative." She looked up and smiled. "That's what's in it, Everett."

"Well, thanks bunch for that," he said. "I have to admit, it is curiously refreshing."

"Don't thank me. I'm still just an apprentice here, which means I've still got a lot to learn about the great healing traditions. Here are your street clothes, Everett. All laundered and pressed." As she spoke, she handed him his pants, then waited without turning away. Then she handed him his shirt and helped him on with his jacket with a charming ladylike smile. "Now, let's get you the Wild Thyme commissary, where the lyceum chefs are all apprentices of the culinary arts. Get ready for a super delicious and healthy buffet brunch, Everett! The gourmet meals here are prepared expressly for guests by the next generation of epicurean masters."

"That sure sounds good to me, Raven," Everett said, adjusting his street clothes. "But what about Mister Brody?" The little lion circled the place they were standing, occasionally brushing up against Raven's beautiful bare legs.

"Ah, that's so sweet and considerate of you, Everett. I'm so happy you would include my little leading man. But don't worry, Mister Brody knows his way around the lyceum commissary, and everyone, including the apprentice builders, scholars, healers, and chefs, simply adores him."

Days at the Wild Thyme lyceum passed by pleasantly, one leading to another, yet an emptiness still filled the poet's heart. Early one morning, gazing up into a patch of brightening blue sky as the sun burned away the veil of maritime fog, Everett caught sight of a majestic hawk flying high overhead, its wings slicing through the cloudless azure sky with ease. This hawk was soon joined by another, and then another, each appearing suddenly from behind the mountain ridge. Everett watched in amazement, fascinated by the fierce calypso movements of the aerial courtship and/or territorial defense. He heard the hawks calling overhead, their distinctive high-pitched shrieks louder than the chattering and tweeting of the forest's songbirds. Later that afternoon, Everett was invited by Raven to help out at the phytochemistry workshop, where she was busy preparing a ceremonial herbal component for the hands-on healing demonstration, of which Everett Durant was the principal subject.

"Prepare yourself to learn something that is both very old and very new, Everett. The finest thing about this place is that all the great healing traditions are included, and no one philosophy is allowed to dominate the others or capture the flag of tradition. It's as simple as watch one, do one, teach one, from this point on," she said, handing Everett a loose-fitting lab coat.

"Count me in," Everett said. He donned the lab coat, turning the collar up for effect.

"I need you to hold this cheesecloth over the paper filter just so"—she showed him how—"as I pour this oil extraction of boswellic acids, commonly known as frankincense, into the center."

"I'm happy to hold and even to squeeze this drippy cheesecloth as needed, Doc. But can you tell me what frankincense has to do with my hands-on healing, without going through too much biochemistry?"

"I'm not a medical doctor, Everett. More like an apprentice of the ancient apothecaries, who emulated the art of the perfumer, or incense maker, by manufacturing a holy oil, an anointing oil, or a healing oil. You can think of this healing balm I'm making specially for you as a musical composition with a mix of themes, principles, and instruments for certain effects."

"Tell me more, Raven. What exactly, in terms of themes, principles, and instruments, blends harmoniously with this frankincense extraction, according to the ancient apothecaries?"

"I'll explain as I understand it, as long as you can concentrate and not drop your end of the cheesecloth until the hot oil stops dripping. The main theme is an anti-inflammatory 'hush' composed of three therapeutic substances from the East. The boswellic acids from frankincense are known to hush inflammation by blocking the activity of 5-lipoxygenase. And I have learned that one should never let acute inflammation become chronic, Everett—so many bad things can happen. In addition to this boswellic acid extraction, I will need to prepare a betulinic acid tincture from birch bark, which hushes nasty oncogenic specificity proteins, and I will need to solubilize some concentrated oleanolic acid, extracted from olive pomace, which hushes hyperactive cytokine storms at the DNA level and hinders the survival of inflammatory bad actors."

"It looks like the cheesecloth just stopped dripping, Raven. What do I do with it now?"

"Time to squeeze. … Yes, tightly, just like that," she instructed him. "Just keep on squeezing."

When they finished filtering the extraction, Raven held up the bottle to the bench light, where a luminous swirl was seen forming in the cooling mixture. Much like rock candy crystals forming in a saturated solution of sugars, the pentacyclic triterpenes were forming into crystalline layers within the carrier oil, reflecting the light. Everett watched Raven with a growing fascination as she moved decisively to label and store the bottle, and then record the procedure.

"How old are you, Raven? If you don't mind my asking. It's just that I'm having trouble even guessing your age in light of your knowledge of botanicals and your youthful appearance."

"I'm much older than I look, Everett Durant, much like Mister Brody. I won't tell you my age just yet, but I will tell you I am old enough to choose a partner in life, and possibly a husband."

The hands-on healing demonstration turned out to be a clinical affair, with Everett lying stark naked on a therapeutic massage table that might as well have been an operating table, or an examination table for a vivisection, or a stone-cold slab, an interim resting place for a cadaver.

The apprentice and the lyceum apothecaries gathered around the table/slab, and the ceremony began with Raven's invocation: "Our therapeutic intention is to reach in deeply, perchance to mend some part of Everett Durant that was lost at sea or was broken when his hopes of a grand love died." The congregation of apprentices formed an even tighter circle around the stone-cold slab. "This evening we will be applying two transdermal balms in sequence. First, we will apply a fast-acting anti-inflammatory composition called Hush Balm directly to Everett's unhealed joints, including his neck and shoulders and all along his spine. After an induction time of approximately ten minutes, the subject will be turned onto his back to receive the long-awaited subterranean Heart Balm, which will be applied directly to his rib cage. The subterranean heart balm is our newest test formulation, containing a clinical-grade tincture of hawthorn leaf with flowers rich in vitexins, and bioactive extracts of horse chestnut, *Bacopa monnieri*, and *Centella asiatica*, presented in a rapidly penetrating and permeating oil base."

The effects of the healing balms came upon Everett Durant symphonically, with the awakening alarm of a marching band—a band led by a fleet of fancy prancing horses, followed by waves of loud brass instruments, cymbals, and drums, made complete with the titillating attractions of high-stepping drum majorettes. Next, a flotilla of rose-covered parade floats came and went with the glamor of dazzling beauty queens, each wearing a jeweled crown that sparkled brightly and each waving aloha to the onlookers, as the flotilla of parade floats passed on by, accompanied by rousing orchestrations, leaving only the somnambulistic sound of silence in its wake.

One by one, all the inflamed joints of the tragic poet's body went dark. All sensations of pain left his limbs, and he was left floating corpse-like in the darkness—and yet he was aware.

Everett could feel his leaden body being physically turned over. He could feel his individual ribs lighting up like fluorescent bulbs, the aching sensations within them reaching the upper limit as he breathed in, and could also feel the pain of his heart, trapped and beating rapidly within the confines of his ill-illuminated rib cage. And then his glowing ribs went dark. As evening fell, he felt his lonely poet's heart struggling to escape its bounds. He felt it flutter and watched it attempt to rise up and fly free into the evening sky in search of something so beautiful and elusive as this endless river of stars.

PART III
EPIC INTERCONTINENTAL CLIFFHANGER

Chapter 7

Yo, Travis here! Remember me? I'm a friend of Everett Durant's from Bonaventure Pointe and a regular surfer with the local dawn patrol. If you are reading this, then you must have been given a formal invitation by the heiress. The invitation I received was an ornately gilded handwritten *note diplomatique*, if you'll pardon my French, requesting the pleasure of my company at the Fabulous Manifesta's latest art house event—can you imagine that? a virtual reality gala staged deep in the Big Sur woods—along with the company of my good buddy Everett Durant, to honor the musical contributions of Celeste Emo. The invitation said that I should contact Captain Jack Raulston of the *Good Ship Pequod* to make travel arrangements for Monterey ASAP. The invitation specifically read: "You are most welcome to bring one or more of your colleagues." So, of course, I invited my friend Monty and my associates from the dawn patrol.

The trip up the coast to Monterey by way of the *Good Ship Pequod* was freaky, to say the least. It took two days of hard sailing amid inclement weather. We were taking spray over the gunnels as we rounded Point Conception, and then all the way to Morro Bay, where the skipper skillfully timed our entrance to and exit from the harbor fuel docks, dicey as it was, maneuvering amid six-foot swells. Traveling at sea past sunset, heading north into stormy weather up along the Big Sur coastline, where you know that there is simply no safe landing—the thought of navigating in darkness still gives me chills. It was some comfort to see Monty's unsinkable inflatable Zodiac trailing behind the *Pequod* on a tow rope, just in case we would need it.

But the company was good, the party was amped, and the catered food in the galley was outstanding—not at all what one would expect for a tour boat on a routine whale-watching trip. Although I have to admit I was relieved to see the lights of Carmel-by-the-Sea in the fog, and I only began to relax when Captain Jack steered the *Good Ship Pequod* around the old lighthouse and entered the safety of Lovers' Point, where we could see the lights of Monterey Harbor.

We were met at the dock by more than a dozen upscale SUVs with tinted windows. We piled into the SUVs with all the refinement of a barrel of monkeys. Then things got serious when the motorcade met up at Carmel Highlands and the flashing lights went on at Castle Rock and we crossed the span of the Bixby Creek Bridge in pitch-darkness. Things got even more serious farther on, when we saw that we were actually passing roadblock barricades in single file on a single, reopened lane. We could see the bulldozers and loaders working with floodlights as we passed by. It was the same way at Hurricane Point—one-way traffic moving in single file in seeming slow motion on a road marked Closed to the Public. Like I said: freaky.

We got there at just the right time, as if somebody could actually plan the timing of our perilous journey by sea and land to the Henry Miller Memorial Library, where everyone was already taking their seats in folding chairs on the lawn or gathering around the circular stage setup, waiting for the Fabulous Manifesta's VR gala in the Big Sur woods. My friends and I mixed in with the gathering crowd. We were all pumped, standing casually by the circular stage, feeling comfortably *backstage,* like on a movie set. We chatted excitedly with the virtual 3D hologram projection guys and gals, who had basically finished setting up the computer-generated laser riggings and controls and were just standing and waiting expectantly for the spectacle to begin.

Everett arrived on the scene shortly after we did, presumably by means of a similar motorcade. I first caught sight of him shaking hands with a group of hooded monks assembled in a tight group around what looked to be a professional DJ mixing table, along with a peculiar-looking young man wearing a bright white "I Heart Jesus" T-shirt under his monk-like hoodie.

Everett and the hooded monks were joined by a bevy of mysterious mademoiselles—clearly Hollywood types—in obvious disguises; to wit, some of them were wearing sunglasses at night. I watched Everett mingle and move easily through the large crowd of his friends, which included a wide polychromatic array of offbeat people—campers, homeless, migrants, wanderers, and vagabonds beyond ordinary description. It was good to see Everett meeting and greeting everyone gathered around to honor the memory and the music of Celeste Emo.

When Everett reached the place where we were standing, a handshake just wasn't good enough: we hugged and fist-bumped and high-fived like there was no tomorrow. For me, it felt like a special occasion. There was clearly something different about the way Everett looked. He looked younger than before, no kidding. He looked less beaten down by life—less downbeat than he had before, if you know what I mean. There was something very different about his general bearing: that faraway look in his eyes was a scintilla less far away, the new look, a scintilla more present.

Everett told Monty and me to fasten our seat belts, so to speak. He said, "The last time Brother I-Heart and these Big Sur monks covered 'Paradise' by Coldplay, it was a landslide event!"

Everett worked his way back to the DJ mixing table, where the hooded monks were assembled offstage, much like background singers at a classical music concert. We saw Everett tuning an acoustic guitar while he was being miked in to the electronic sound system. That's when the rhythmic tech trance house music began to pound out in earnest. In a matter of minutes, everyone in the audience was up and moving to the compelling techno beat, which sounded like hypnotic human voices echoing through the wilderness.

The rising orchestral chords that followed were soaring, and impressively loud considering the remote location. Brother I-Heart, the DJ, used the synthesizers and controllers, along with the choir of hooded monks, to layer Coldplay's original threads and vocals and form a mystifying, mesmerizing rave-style trance music that continued on and on with its postpunk / techno / new wave synth mix—simply amazing. It reminded me a lot of an electronic music festival I'd gone to a few years back at the Waterfront Park in San Diego, where PK extended the catchy threads of Jefferson Airplane's "White Rabbit" like forever, utilizing haunting iconic *Alice in Wonderland* vocals. This particular evening, Brother I-Heart et al. and this extended techno version of "Paradise" just kept going and going, the way good dance music does.

By the time the set ended, we were pretty much warmed up, despite the evening's being chilly and uncertain with a thick maritime fog moving in. The opening set was followed by a mysterious mademoiselle with sunglasses who strode calmly onto the stage to make an appealing public announcement. We were informed that a rally was being organized in Monterey and Santa Cruz to peacefully protest against the federal moratorium on whale disentanglement efforts, amounting to an official lockdown on any kind of humane rescue. Now, we were all well aware of the actual cause of the problem: fishing and crabbing gear in all the wrong places. However, thanks to this late-night public announcement, we were made aware of the extreme urgency—a crisis happening right here, right now, in the deep-sea feeding grounds right off Monterey Bay.

As it happens, unlike chronological or sequential time, which we all live our lives by, there exists in classical rhetoric—and in surfing, I should add—a passing instant called *kairos*, an opportune moment when an opening appears that one must drive forcefully through if one is to achieve any kind of success. I felt something like that when I looked over to see what Everett Durant was up to and I noticed that the DJ with the "I Heart Jesus" T-shirt was leaning in close to him and whispering something, with Everett, listening, smiling and nodding as if in agreement.

I was discussing the matter with Monty and Kristin when a second warm-up act was announced. We all heard the deep resonating bass sounds of an electronic voice-over and the Fabulous Manifesta's signature audiovisual stepwise countdown beginning with a startling acoustic blare. The dramatically over-the-top introduction was supposed to showcase the next-generation talented up-and-coming female vocalist who was scheduled to sing, but things didn't go well.

Whether it was the awesomeness of the audiovisual effects or the onset of a paralyzing stage fright at the worst possible time, it was a hard thing to watch. The young woman with the guitar simply froze like an icicle while the opening chords of the sleeper hit "Let Her Go" by Passenger repeated again and again like a broken record.

That's when Everett Durant sprang into action. He agilely leapt up with his acoustic guitar and headed to center stage. Smiling confidently, he stared tenderly into the eyes of the petrified diva, then picked up on the guitar lead-in and sang the first verse all by himself.

"'Well, you only need the light when it's burning low. / Only know you love her when you let her go.'" He sang the opening lines for the young singer. It was touching. Thankfully, her fear melted, and she dove into the next verse with the voice of an angel, singing the part about staring at the bottom of a glass, hoping one day to make a dream last. It was as if we could all see Celeste Emo when we closed our eyes. Even without understanding why, we knew that everything we touched would surely die. It was that kind of cover song.

"Because you loved her too much and you dove too deep" was the sublime message behind the lyrics. No wonder the original track shot to the top of the charts like a bullet.

This audiovisual re-creation of a Celeste Emo concert was wondrous, to be sure. The use of CGI mapping on an invisible reflective foil screen only served to enhance the eeriness of the Big Sur setting, with voice, gesture, music, lighting, and special effects working together to capture the high points of Celeste Emo's legendary career. With each familiar song, the visual experience morphed from virtual reality to augmented reality with Manifesta's state-of-the-art techno holographs. Still, I couldn't help but wonder what Everett was really thinking about all this. Even at the peak of the 3D holographic gala, which featured a stunning series of Celeste Emo arias and a mesmerizing digital avatar of Everett Durant, I got the impression that something vital was missing here and that the experience was considerably lesser than that at a real live show.

We all got together after the concert to discuss the present situation in Monterey Bay. Was this going to be a sociopolitical statement along the lines of *Free Willy*, or something bigger?

Chapter 8

We all started out with Everett Durant on the *Good Ship Pequod* well before dawn, which is far and away my favorite time of the day. Monterey Bay was calm when we headed out. The sea beyond the bay had calmed substantially during the night, with only light winds coming from the northwest and the fog lifting. The urgent cries of the herring gulls following us out of the harbor were drowned out by the long, low wail of a foghorn that sounded out its repeated warning every few minutes from the breakwaters of the Coast Guard Pier.

Captain Jack had been talking with the local whale disentanglement organization at Cannery Row while we were all busy celebrating with Everett Durant at the 3D holographic diva show. Captain Jack told us the scuttlebutt when we boarded the *Pequod*. Right here in Monterey Bay they had a team of well-trained, well-prepared, perfectly capable *hombres* and *mujeres*, all frozen in an awful overwhelming time, frozen just like the icicle diva onstage. The local heroes were temporarily forbidden from participating, but they had the right gear to disentangle the whale.

Regardless of the disputed cause of this particular humpback whale's entanglement in the floats and fishing gear, and regardless of the ineffectual solutions currently provided—short of outright disentangling the whale—the official would-be cetacean rescue teams were, each and every one, unable to move fast, to think past, or to act because of the federal moratorium. It was a terrifying imposition of enforced social, political, and cultural inactivity, if you ask me. It was a prime example of intentional overbearing underhanded overreach, if you ask me.

If you were to ask Captain Jack, you'd get the same answer. Captain Jack would be thinking of freeing the stricken humpback whale and its calf, which was bravely facing the catastrophe.

We spotted the entangled whale and its calf easily enough with GPS and the help of local whale spotters, who had gotten up early. We could see that the great leviathan was seriously entangled, judging by the number of lines and floats streaming from both her mouth area and her tail. The exhausted mother humpback was moving slow enough for us to easily keep up with her, enabling us to see what exactly had to be done and where precisely to cut the lines, if doing that was even possible.

We all had our own ideas of what to do, yet we had only one real option. Monty was already putting on his wet suit when we all realized the same thing. Kristin looked frightfully worried, like I had never seen her before. Everett was busy with some kind of boat hook contraption, lashing the Captain Hook cutting edge to use as an extension for the aluminum poles. There was not much more for a surf dude to do, and there was nothing my friends in the dawn patrol could contribute beyond watching the whale. But there was no way that I was going to miss this epic West Coast Nantucket sleighride by just standing there on the tour boat.

I was the first one into the inflatable Zodiac when the *Pequod* slowed down and Monty and Everett Durant reeled it in. We must have looked like the knightly spirit of old Don Quixote himself with our long, extended lances held high against the threatening windmills of monstrous misfortune. For me, there was a new and heroic part of the equation, yet Monty was already in the zone. And Everett was hard to read, especially when the Zodiac was moving fast.

Monty was a master at maneuvering the light powerboat in rough waters and dicey spaces, and we were soon close enough to the humpback's tail section to begin cutting the lines from her flesh. The Captain Hook cutting edges on the pole extensions enabled us to reach out and cut the thick lines with precision, leaving only deep gashes visible in the whale's skin, with some blubber showing.

Monty kept pace with the female humpback, steering the Zodiac close in and away from the calf.

I turned to look behind us, and I caught sight of the ghostlike form of a US Coast Guard cutter bearing down. In the confusion, I saw that the *Good Ship Pequod* had stopped to retrieve the floats and the fishing gear the whale had become entangled in, presumably to be hauled onboard like flotsam by the dutiful watermen of the Bonaventure Pointe Dawn Patrol.

The dark gray hump of the female leviathan loomed up before us as large as a billboard, exposing her knobby ridges and her scars. The Zodiac was moving slow enough for us to see a remaining entangled object deep in her mouth, with a raft of thick ropes and riggings with floats pulled tight against her jawbone and caught on her pectoral flipper. The situation looked grim.

Monty maneuvered in close enough to touch the old girl as we pressed into position, where we were eye to eye with the whale.

If you have never looked into an eye that is that much larger than your own, you should. Anyway, we did. Monty and Everett and me, that is. Slowly, in one majestic blink of that ginormous lady humpback eye, there was an astounding awareness that became evident to me. The lady leviathan blinked at us, who were desperately trying to help her. One beauteous wink showing her *awareness* of sea and sky, and pain and life, and suffering. We all saw it! If I had to describe it in the terms of virtual and/or artificial reality, I'd say it was an awareness that was toggled to share.

We looked at each other desperately, not questioning whether this was the right moment, just knowing that our time had arrived. Monty simply nodded to Everett, who moved quickly to replace him at the helm. Monty detached the wrist strap, with a lanyard leading to the engine cutoff switch, from his wrist—a safety device called a kill switch that immediately shuts off the outboard motor if the helmsman becomes separated from the boat's controls—and threw it over to me as he grabbed hold of a Captain Hook pole extension and moved to the side of the powerboat, where he pointed to the tangled raft of rope and floats, shouting, "Closer! Closer!" And then he was over the side.

She was more than fifty feet long and at least as many tons in the water by my estimation. The danger to life and limb was vastly apparent—even more so considering that the whale was injured. Nevertheless, Monty dove bravely forth onto the tangled raft, where he moved on his hands and knees, under the watch of the whale's enormous eyeball, toward the nexus of tangles near the corner of her mouth and her pectoral fin. It was hard enough for me to make out what Monty was even doing, let alone ponder what he was thinking, when he climbed his way up into the morass of tangles at the mouth of the lady leviathan and began to wield his specialized cutting instrument like a crazed dentist wielding a drill.

Suddenly a discernable *pop* was heard. The lady humpback's mouth opened wide and closed, and I temporarily lost sight of Monty. I was sure glad to see him emerge in one piece amid the massive stream of entanglements. He was still holding onto the cutting pole when the raft of flotsam separated from the humpback. She breached, then she dived, disappearing, along with her uninjured calf, back into the sea.

And we let her go.

*   *   *

Back aboard the *Good Ship Pequod*, everyone's eyes were riveted to the large, sharp, imposing bow of the great white US Coast Guard cutter that was still approaching, less than a mile away, with its big radar beacon, and a flag, and a man on the rail. The cutter had numbers on the side. It just kept on coming, and it didn't look like it was here to deliver the mail.

We were all surprised when an amplified voice boomed out over a loudspeaker. "Ahoy there, captain of the *Pequod*!" Surprisingly, it was a woman's voice. It sure brought Captain Jack out onto the deck in a hurry. "O captain, my captain!" the unseen voice boomed. "How in the world can I even begin thank you?!" she queried, sounding a lot less threatening and a lot more inviting this time. "How about a romantic dinner for two in Monterey?!"

When we heard that suggestive invitation, we all started cheering and celebrating right along with Captain Jack. Monty filled us in on the details of the love affair between Captain Jack and Doctor Jessica, the beautiful, bountiful marine research scientist with deep-dish PhD credentials, while Captain Jack finished dancing and spinning on deck like a madman, waving his arms up at the imposing bow of the coast guard cutter. We all motored back to Monterey feeling like seaworthy sailors as the sun climbed higher in the sky.

What was supposed to be a public gathering for peaceful protesting—against the constraints of a misguided moratorium with its fatalistic lockdown—turned into an all-day, all-night block festival: a celebration of unanticipated social responsibilities, shared intuitions, and outright civil nonconformity, which began to take the shape and size of a much larger cultural occasion. By the time we rounded the breakwaters of Monterey Harbor, beaming like champions returning from a harrowing death-defying ordeal, we were big news. The whole thing was captured on film with digital cameras and was streamed live on the internet. And that's how the captain and crew of the *Good Ship Pequod* became the focal point of the festivities at Old Fisherman's Wharf.

I was told that this was once a commercial fishing pier serving Cannery Row, that is, before John Steinbeck's seedy local characters, like the sardines, were driven out to the point of extinction. Old Fisherman's Wharf was now an upscale shopping and entertainment venue with ocean-themed specialty shops: gift shops featuring nautical souvenirs, jewelry stores with silver and pearls in the windows, and candy shops, some pulling saltwater taffy on-location, others with candy apples on a stick in the windows, glossy red and inviting, or covered with thick caramel and coconut flakes.

One by one, the shuttered doors of the Cannery Row gift shops were opened wide to us, the returning heroes. And people generously gave us gifts. In no time at all, glossy color prints of the Zodiac-powered rescue mission—the ones where we had our knightly Don Quixote lances held high—arrived on the party scene. And Monty, our whale-riding hero, was mobbed. He was mobbed with attention and was attempting to sign a slew of souvenir photographs with a Sharpie, while a gaggle of fervent new female admirers were pressing in upon him.

Just one look at Kristin observing the mob scene around Monty, with her swimsuit model's body and her practiced mean-girl standoffishness showing as she watched the other young women interacting with him, and I could tell that her attitude had changed for the better. There was a new fervor to the body language she was exhibiting, knowing that Monty's stature had risen both in the relationship and in the community.

Not to be outdone by the owners of the gift shops and the jewelry shops, a number of the owners of the upscale seafood restaurants located on the boardwalks and piers of Old Fisherman's Wharf opened up their kitchens for the special occasion. The celebration grew even larger in size, the spontaneous festivities morphing from free lunch for the returning heroes in the early afternoon to a complimentary dinner honoring those who had tilted like Don Quixote all through the night.

I sampled everything: simple fish and chips and a milkshake; steaming hot clam chowder served in a bread bowl; red snapper broiled over a wood fire, stuffed with spiced tomatoes, and garnished with seasonal vegetables; a seafood sampler with breaded crab cakes, grilled ginger-lime scallops, and crab Louie with mixed greens, not to mention the divine desserts: vanilla sponge cake tiramisu, chocolate dream layer cake, warm apple pie, and silky-smooth crème brûlée served with espresso coffee. All these flavors were combined with the heady ambience created by the alternative techno pop music, the all-night dancing with perfect strangers, and the phantasmagoria of colorful lights and shimmering images that were playing upon the water.

I lost sight of Captain Jack early in the evening, with all the frenzied dining and dancing and celebrating going on nonstop. I can only presume that he hooked up with Jessica for some high-level discussion of nautical maps and charts with protractors that measure in degrees those private places where lovers roll and toss, engaged in meaningful acts of love in the briny deep.

I finally caught up with Everett Durant sometime around midnight. I remember him clearly. Standing alone with the lights reflecting blurrily off Old Fisherman's Wharf, Everett looked different to me from how he had looked back then, before he went off on a road trip with the gossamer heiress, as Everett referred to her. Back then, he had the forlorn look of a man whose tears had been all used up on another love—a hard-to-let-go-of kind of love.

But here he was, telling me about some beauty named Raven and a little lion named Brody he had befriended in a valley with heavenly lights. In the brief time we spent together at the party, Everett told me a wild story about being on a helicopter and parachuting into LA's mean streets, where angels fear to tread. Then, alternatively, they flew like bats into the dark tunnels of an underground railroad and/or sailing on a ship named *Fram* that led him to a surrealistic three-ring circus in a nightmare world where amazing acrobats flew high overhead and a hot-air balloon came crashing down into a cornfield where a Native American roadman drove up in an old Apache pickup truck. It was all a bit much, but I loved hearing about it and seeing him.

I saw Everett Durant again the very next day. He was standing on the floating docks at the Coast Guard Pier, where the *Good Ship Pequod* was honorarily moored. He was talking with Monty and Kristin, who had decided to remain in Monterey for a few days and were now shifting their luggage and other gear from the *Pequod* into the tiny Zodiac. It turned out that Monty's unsinkable Zodiac powerboat was already an *objet d'art,* gleaming as a curiosity with celebrity, and new value, having appreciated more in value overnight than a classic car in the Pebble Beach Concours d'Elegance. Already, scuttlebutt was circulating around greater Monterey about casting a new bronze statue for the Cannery Row collection of monuments to diverse individuals, adding the Zodiac and its knights, cast in bronze, as a permanent monument to honor us for our courageous act of ecological and civil disobedience.

The idea of a new bronze statue was too delightful for me to even imagine. At the moment, it was more interesting and entertaining for me to watch the beautiful, glamorous waitress and mean girl Kristin strutting her stuff like a peacock in Carmel, with her stunning SoCal swimsuit model's body pressed up close against my friend Monty, with her slender arms wrapped tightly, around this real live hero of her own.

I could see a soft, sweet look in Kristin's eyes as she smiled and waved up to me. Everett helped Monty and Kristin load the Zodiac, and the happy couple motored back toward the harbor town.

"Hey, Travis!" Everett shouted, as he climbed up from the floating docks to join me on the pier.

"Hey, yo, Everett," I said in response. "It's really good to see you looking so sprightly, dude." I shook him. "We were all pretty worried about you and your little road trip with Miss Beatrice. Especially when we hadn't heard anything from you. And then we heard about the landslides and road closures along the Big Sur coastline, and I feared that your road trip with the gossamer heiress might turn out to be another disappointing adventure in the larger story of your life."

"I was a bit worried myself for a while," he said. "But I found that Miss Beatrice is an excellent designated driver with refined tastes in alternative music and an appetite for high adventure."

"What actually happened to you, Everett? You told me some wild things last night, but just look at you! You're not even limping anymore. And you look a whole lot happier." I looked him over carefully as he moved easily along the boardwalk. "Egad, man, you even look younger!"

"Thanks for noticing that, Travis. I do feel a whole lot better these days." Everett fake-frowned, and then he tap-danced on the boardwalk and spun around wildly like a flamenco dancer. "Do I really look that much different to you?"

"Yes, Everett, you do look different! You no longer look to me like that tortured, beaten-down Professor Sad I once knew, that poetic dreamer who could only find his way in the moonlight, only to find himself being punished for being so visionary as to see the dawning of something new and beautiful before the rest of the world could see it. That's what you told me, as I recall."

"Well, now that you mention it, I should probably modify that story for you, Travis."

As we strolled along the Coast Guard Pier, he told me, "This poetic phrase describing the punishment of the idealistic dreamer—as was penned by Oscar Wilde in his essay 'The Critic as Artist'—requires a deeper, fuller explanation for such a thoughtful surf dude as you. According to Mr. Wilde—and here I must agree—the punishment of the romantic dreamer is also his reward, as revealed in the dialogue found within the essay."

I asked him, "Can you tell me more about this reward clause as it relates to your looking so spry?"

He told me straight out: "The road trip in the moonlight with the gossamer heiress turned out to be a real gift, Travis. The reward for me personally was that I got a glimpse behind the proverbial curtain, a glimpse of extraordinary vistas, exotic locations, and intellectual insights from her exceedingly resourceful, cultured, influential, and high-minded point of view."

Everett stopped walking forward, and he turned to face me as he spoke. "In return for a simple lyrical suggestion I once made to her in Bonaventure Pointe, which worked out well, Miss Beatrice concocted this entire surrealistic road trip for me as an opportunity to learn, to heal, and to participate in something marvelous, important, and totally underground, including my own hands-on healing experience, which I really didn't expect."

Recalling our unscripted Nantucket sleighride experience, which was still fresh in my mind, I had to ask: "I certainly didn't expect to find myself bow-surfing on a humpback whale with you and Monty, hacking away at lines and riggings that didn't belong there in the first place. Tell me this, Everett: what exactly did that curious monk with the 'I Heart Jesus' T-shirt whisper into your ear at the gala, right after the public announcement about the moratorium?"

We stopped walking. I caught Everett's gaze and looked directly into his eyes, waiting for his answer. I didn't expect him to answer, but he did.

"The young fellow with the expressive T-shirt is a next-generation apprentice monk, Travis. Brother I-Heart simply reminded me that all creatures of the land and the sea rightly belong to the one who would save them. It's really not a big secret," he said. Then he looked far off into the distance.

We continued walking and reminiscing until we reached the end of the boardwalk of the Coast Guard Pier. Beyond the edge of the boat dock, a rock pile extended out to form the breakwater of the harbor. It was still early morning when we turned around and headed back to the *Pequod*. I could see my dawn patrol buddies were gathering, waiting for the boat's captain.

"What are you not telling me, Everett?"

"A lot," he admitted with a smile. "However, what I can tell you, with some assurance, is that there is a young surf dude, Travis, who is in deep trouble medically speaking, and I am reminded that the lovely Miss Beatrice circulates in a land of legends and lore, socializing with amazing intellectuals and astonishing healers who openly tend to the wounded under fire."

"A young surf dude in deep trouble? That's rich, Everett," I said, scolding him soundly. "That could mean a lot of things to a lot of people," I told him. "Deep medical trouble, you say? It could be anybody!"

"Exactly!" he said. Then he stopped in midstride and turned to me, announcing, "And that's why I'm heading back into the Big Sur wilderness, Travis. Lately it occurs to me that my road trip is still in progress. Although my life in the fast lane appears to have slowed to the measured pace of a forest walk, I still have much left to learn, even at my advanced age."

"I still can't get over how much younger you look—and how much healthier! Even your eyes look younger," I told him. We laughed, and then I asked him, "So you finally found what you were looking for so desperately and so long? Do you think you might start writing songs again?"

"I still don't know much, Travis. And I can't say if I will ever write songs like before. Heaven knows, Stella live, as Celeste Emo, was always the melody in the music for me—still is. Her voice brought the love songs to life." Everett paused as a cloud of emotion passed over his face, then he continued. "There is something very special happening at this lyceum of cultural rehabilitation, continuing adult education, and participation that I told you about last night. It's much like Sugar Mountain in the song. There are lots of young people there, at the fair, with the barkers and the colored balloons. And there are lots of older people with wisdom, who are still young at heart. It's a happening place, Travis. And you are always welcome at my campfire!"

We both laughed. I said, "You can tell me more about this lyceum concept on our sea voyage back to Bonaventure Pointe. It looks to me like Captain Jack has just arrived on the scene."

"Listen, Travis. I won't be heading back with you guys on the *Good Ship Pequod* today. I realize now that there is so much more for me to learn and to do in terms of providing refuge, care, and purpose for the homeless and the hopeless. I would appreciate it if you would look after my cottage until I return, perhaps in the fall, surely less than a month of Sundays from today."

We shook hands and bumped knuckles, and that was the last time I saw Everett Durant.

*   *   *

Heading home, sailing down the California coast with a following wind, I couldn't help but think about all the tragic things that had happened to Everett Durant and the way he responded to them. He told me that he was heading back to the valley of the heavenly lights, at least for a while. He told me he realized he still had a lot more to learn and, possibly, something more to share with others.

For me, it felt good to be heading home. I miss everything about *the Pointe,* as Everett fondly referred to it. If you ever get a chance to experience the endearing and enchanting headlands of Bonaventure Pointe from the vantage point of the Pacific Ocean—even if it's for the very first time—you'll understand why you came this way.

Printed in the United States
by Baker & Taylor Publisher Services